ALSO BY STEPHANIE MIRRO

THE LAST PHOENIX
Wings of Fire
Wings of Winter
Wings of Magic
Wings of Life
Wings of Deceit
Wings of Mercy

IMMORTAL RELICS
Curse of the Vampire
Fury of the Gods
Revenge of the Witch
Rise of the Demons

COLLECTIONS
The Outsiders: An Hourlings Anthology

WINGS OF WINTER

THE LAST PHOENIX: BOOK THREE

STEPHANIE MIRRO

TANNHAUSER PRESS

Dedication

For Sydney and Amber.
A sister by blood and a sister by choice.
Your love and support keep me going on the darkest days.

AUTHOR'S NOTE

The phoenix language introduced in this book is not intended to be a direct translation of Russian. As with most languages, dialects form and differentiate themselves from others, often based on geographical changes and time passing. Because Russian is a derivative of the phoenix tongue based on an introduction millennia ago, it therefore makes sense that it would not be identical.

Also, this is a fantasy book. Thank you for your understanding!

CHAPTER 1

Tuesday Afternoon

It was down to him or me, and I was not going down without a fight.

I steadied my right hand, pinning down the gift-wrapped package, and reached for the tape dispenser, never moving my eyes from the target. I had been at this task for at least five minutes now, also known as an eternity.

But of course, it could never be a simple job.

The dispenser tipped over with a thump, mocking me with its distance from my fingers. A bead of sweat threatened to obscure my vision—less from this sad attempt and more from the desert's summer heat. I leaned farther, stretching as much as I could without losing my grip on the package. My fingers brushed the device once. Twice.

Third time's the charm.

Triumph roared through me as I slapped a strip of Scotch tape across the brown paper reserved for such attempts, forever wrapping the newly purchased book in place. Until the recipient opened it, anyway. I shoved the mess of a wrapped gift into the customer's reusable cloth bag and looked up, a please-don't-ask-me-to-redo-it smile plastered across my face. Because the next time was sure to be worse.

"Here you go," I said to the grey-haired customer. She gave me an odd look behind thick-lensed glasses before muttering a thanks. The bell chimed above the glass front door as she left. Outside the shop's window, the woman peeked inside the bag and shook her head.

I winced. I didn't blame her reaction one bit.

Yes, this was my life now: feigning excitement over selling dead trees to people and wrapping them in even more dead trees like some sort of cannibalistic ritual. Books and I had never really gotten along, thanks to the challenges of dyslexia, so it was anyone's guess why I thought working at a bookstore of all places was a good idea.

Since no one was around to see, I rolled my eyes. Oh yeah, to hide from an army of bounty hunters after a set-for-life kind of payday. I brushed a strand of dark brown hair out of my face, glaring at it because it wasn't my normal white-blonde. Not that it was my hair's fault for being brown—no, that blame belonged to a shit-for-brains fae necromancer—but it was better than taking out my frustration on an unsuspecting bookstore customer.

I focused on tidying up the counter. Crumpled bits of brown wrapping paper and sticky tape littered the surface from other attempts today. Wrapping gifts was a skill I did not possess, nor would I have ever chosen to possess it had I not been exiled from my previous life.

Only a month had passed since leaving Miami, also known as paradise, for Tucson, also known as hell. Okay, to be fair—maybe it was just purgatory. Some people chose to be here, for generations even. And to be even more fair, I wasn't actually banished or exiled, it just wasn't safe for me to return to Miami right now.

The delightful owner of Antigone Books, the eclectic 4th Avenue downtown Tucson bookstore, gave me a job stocking shelves and ringing up customers, never the wiser that it was merely a distraction to keep me from getting bored enough to do something stupid—also known as my specialty. Day after day, I rang people up, wasting away while waiting for news from my witchy best friend, or my grim reaper pseudo partner at the Death Enforcement Agency, or even my guardian angel. *Someone* needed to call me before I went batshit crazy.

I also held a strong flair for the dramatic.

Don't get me wrong—Tucson was pretty damn cool, with lots of history I knew nothing about and a weird mishmash of people. It had only rained once while I was here, but it left behind the strangest scents, which had me getting weird looks from the locals when I sniffed the air. After I commented on it to a random restaurant server, he explained it was the smell of wet mesquite trees and creosote bushes. I had no idea what either of those were, but I took his word for it.

But even with the neat oddities to keep me distracted, it wasn't home. It wasn't even green. Greys and browns seemed to make up the whole town. And worse, there was no Community presence, which was the reason this locale was chosen to be my hiding place. But I had absolutely nobody to talk to about what was *really* going on in the world, like the possibility of a rising zombie apocalypse courtesy of a maniacal unseelie fae.

I even missed my previous job as a barista at The Morning Grind, serving espresso to regulars like Joe. I'd almost be okay dealing with Isaac's bullshit again. Come to think of it, did he ever officially fire me? I wouldn't know since I didn't have my phone, and I was banned from using the internet while in Tucson.

Oh well. At least the overwhelming woodsy, pulpy smell of new books permeating the store no longer bothered me. I sighed. My brother would have loved it.

"Don't worry, Maddie," Ashley's singsong voice cut through the silence, "you'll get the hang of it all soon."

The petite blonde girl rocking bright blue eyes and a killer tan was the typical all-American do-gooder. Top of her class when she graduated high school. Studying for her bar exams now. She probably should have looked down on a woman like me, a twenty-seven-year-old corporate career failure turned barista turned part-time book stocker, except she was too goddamn nice to look down on anyone. I would miss her when I was finally allowed to return home. Or maybe I would convince her to come with me. Miami would definitely need lawyers more than this place.

"If only to prove you right." As she popped around one of the shelves, I grinned and tucked the tape dispenser back into its place near the register.

It wasn't Ashley's fault she didn't know who I really was. For starters, Maddie wasn't even my real name. But part of my escape to the desert included keeping my identity under wraps until one sexier-than-sin grim reaper came galloping in on a white horse—or, more likely, teleported in—to throw me over a shoulder and haul me home. I'd even take a spanking, a thought that sent a tingle of excitement through my body. I clenched my legs together and shut that feeling down real quick.

Or I would stay until I got bored enough to stop following the rules. It could go either way with my track record.

"Got any plans this weekend?" she asked. "There's a concert at the Hotel Congress. The place is haunted, you know, and a bunch of my friends will be there." Her blue eyes sparkled with mischief.

"Ashley, are you trying to help this old bird make friends?" I slid the scissors back into the drawer beneath the rusty cash register, which flaunted raised metal keys. The old-time behemoth was there simply to add to the store's charm since we used a tablet and chip reader these days. But now the counter looked good as new, and with any luck, no one else would ask me to wrap their books for them.

Ever.

"I know you've only been in town for, what? A month?" she asked but didn't pause for me to confirm, "But there's tons of fun to be had in this city if you know where to look."

I grimaced. "Am I that obvious?"

She laughed. "Even the dead would know you don't like it here. The desert's not for everyone."

Goosebumps rose along my arms at her mention of the dead. Little did she know that the dead were Rising, en masse.

I attempted a smile to hide my discomfort. "It's a neat place, but I'm sure my wandering soul will call me away again someday soon. I'll do my best to enjoy it while I'm here. When are you guys meeting up?"

While she rambled on about her friends and the infamous Hotel Congress, my thoughts drifted away. Madison Fox, the pseudonym I had taken on here in Tucson, was a nomad, moving from place to place, city to city as the wind called her name ever onward.

In reality, Veronica Neill, the real me, was the last phoenix and in hiding to save my ass from all the bounty hunters after my hide—or feathers, in my case. Not to mention Bill the Necromancer probably wanted to make me pay for ruining his night of entertainment and blowing up all his Risen—as in necromancers' walking corpse creations that tried to eat people—and revealing his hideout.

I hid a snicker behind a cough. Oops.

True night had fallen by the time Ashley and I locked up the shop and headed our separate ways. She would drive home to the 'burbs, and I would walk to my apartment in the teeny tiny downtown district. I picked a place only a half-mile from the store for convenience, while also feeling a little like I was home in Florida with the taller surrounding buildings. They really didn't even come close to Miami's high rises, but I appreciated them for trying.

Flickering streetlamps and neon business signs lit the way home, and there were plenty of people still out and about in this part of town where tattoo parlors, hip bars, and wide-ranging knickknack shops all shared real estate. I tucked my hands into my slacks' pockets as I walked, doing my best to enjoy this small bit of normalcy. In recent years, the city had poured money into revitalizing the downtown area, adding a streetcar and decorating everything (including trash cans) with pretty, desert-themed designs. Copper, turquoise, and cacti everywhere you looked.

The shops in this area were brightly painted, too, some with giant murals sprawled across entire walls, reminding me a bit of home. But cacti, sparse trees, and scrubby shrubs were the only greenery in the otherwise barren landscape. I missed the towering palm trees, freshly mowed grass, and bushes gone wild. The ocean and the salty breezes, even the thickness of the humidity. This dry air had my skin thirsting for lotion day in and day out.

I waved to the giant stone warrior head at The Hut as I passed. The statue of a moai saved from a mini-golf course now protected the entrance to a bar. I had yet to try the place out, but I found kinship with the fake monolithic head as we were both outsiders here in the desert.

Did I mention I was going stir-crazy?

I passed a few more bars on my way to the underpass, a road which dipped below the train tracks above. The pass would spit me back out onto the only other real bar hopping streets in this city—Congress and Broadway. My place was on Broadway, the next road over. The underpass was mostly empty of people tonight, except for a couple walking hand in hand on the other side of the short tunnel, and a guy heading toward me in a baseball hat and jacket, probably aiming for 4th Avenue. Since I never wore headphones, the constant hum of the light fixtures and the *whoosh* from cars passing by became the music of the night.

June meant it was hot in Tucson. Like, hitting triple digits on most days. I didn't mind the heat, just the dryness, and it made the nighttime air super enjoyable. The desert had this habit of dipping thirty or more degrees overnight. Still, no one in their right mind would find it cold right now, not even cool enough to wear a jacket, except this guy in his hat passing me on his way for a drink or maybe heading home. I didn't think much of him or his jacket until I recognized the faint tingle of otherness as we passed each other.

I stopped and blinked. What the fuck? I spun around, just catching sight of his muddy boot as he disappeared out the other side of the underpass.

A Community member.

CHAPTER 2

Tuesday Night

My heart beat wildly against my ribs, and I fought with indecision. To go after him and find out why another supernatural Community member was here in a city where I should have been alone, or keep my head down and go home, hoping he didn't notice me. The smart thing was to keep on walking and not ask questions.

But fuck that. I was done with smart.

As I raced back the way I came, my shoes slapped the cement, echoing across the now empty underpass. Even though it was dark out, my enhanced phoenix vision picked up heat signatures, but there was still no sign of him. I ran up 4th Avenue and glanced down each dark side street, peering into parked car windows and ignoring the odd looks

I got from the few people I passed. A warm, fast breeze whipped my hair into my face.

Where the fuck did he go?

A heavy hand fell on my shoulder. I grabbed it, shoved my hips and butt backward, and flipped the assailant over my body. He landed with a grunt on his back. Before he had a chance to recover, I was straddling his chest, my forearm pressed to his throat. Only then did I realize this wasn't my guy—just a plain old human who didn't look old enough to buy a lottery ticket.

"Let me go," he sputtered.

I pushed off him and held out a hand to help him up. Instead, he rubbed his throat and glared at me, scooting away on the sidewalk.

"Jesus, I was just going to ask if you needed help." He got to his feet. "I didn't know you were a crazy lady."

I laughed. "What kind of an idiot thinks it's okay to come up behind someone *at night* and put a hand on them?"

He shook his head at me and backed away, muttering something about me being a bitch.

"Yeah, yeah, get mad at me for your bruised ego." I rolled my eyes and let him go. He wasn't my guy and definitely not worth the fight. I hadn't even lost my breath. Chances were I had overreacted a wee bit, but I was used to living in a crime-filled big city. More than one gun had been pulled on me back home. This was small-town living in the wild west, a surprise around every turn.

After glancing up and down the street one last time, I knew this search was futile. The Community member had gotten away. My gaze drifted toward the cloudless black sky, dotted with a handful of bright stars and the crescent moon winking back at me.

Well, he had gotten away from my *human* form.

I strode quickly down the avenue toward the next side street, my heart beating faster as my excitement grew. I promised my best friend Kit I wouldn't shift into my falcon form unless it was life or death. I turned down the side street leading away from the lights and sounds of Tucson's nightlife, chewing on my lip while I thought through my predicament.

Could I consider this life or death? The guy in the underpass hadn't threatened me in any way. Hell, he didn't even seem to notice me, a fact which got me thinking—did I imagine his otherness? Did a month away from anything supernatural make me feel something that wasn't real?

Nah.

But what business would a Community member have here in Tucson? Was it just a random stop on his way somewhere else? A coincidence? Kit would probably kill me, but I didn't believe in coincidence.

At this moment, anyway.

Convinced I had a solid argument if I needed one, I glanced around to make sure I was alone. I ducked behind a parked car, shifted into my bird form, and took to the dry desert skies. Shifting was an instantaneous experience; my human shape and everything I wore or carried moved into an alternate, static dimension while my falcon came out to play. Talk about convenience.

Dazhbog above, I had missed this feeling. The warm night breeze caressed the red and orange feathers beneath my wings, and I closed my eyes for the briefest moment just to soar. To soak it all in, in case it was the last time again for who knew how long. Anyone looking up from the ground would see little more than a pretty bird's feathers spread out above them before disappearing into the dark. I longed to screech out my excitement at finally getting to fly again, but I had a hunt to focus on, and the last thing I needed was attention.

Dropping my gaze, I took in the ultraviolet lights of the city with my avian vision. Even in the dark, all the colors of the rainbow flared out below me, a mesmerizing symphony of hues that revealed so much more than human eyes ever could. Such a shame for this drab town—drab compared to Miami, anyway. I swooped toward the underpass before wheeling around and retracing our steps.

Ultraviolet lights would reveal any Community member hidden among the humans. All Community species had unique signatures, and I had come to know most of them during my jobs in Miami. Back before I found myself banished to Tucson, when I had been an acquirer of fantastical goods. A re-acquirer, technically, as I ensured magical goods didn't remain in human hands. Only I hadn't been super moral about it all, which got me labeled as a thief.

No hard feelings because it was the truth—and I was fucking good at stealing—except my last big job found me about to become a Master Vampire's next meal or sex slave until the angels finally stepped in. Long story made short: one of their grim reapers had gone rogue and tried to pin a murder and stolen soul on me. Talk about a crazy lady.

Oh, and the Archangel of Miami, as in the head of the local Death Enforcement Agency, knew I was innocent all along but used me as bait.

After that, I had given up my life of danger until one foxy-as-fuck grim reaper named Thane Munro convinced me to work with him on the necromancer case. Which turned out to be the worst idea ever since now I wanted to have his babies, except that scenario was impossible. As a reaper, the man was sterile, and the phoenix mating ritual didn't allow for in vitro fertilization. Magic and science didn't always see eye to eye.

My life had turned into a bad movie. It was almost like—

Wait, what was that?

I dipped a wing and flew back around. There—a black hole amid the ultraviolet lights inside a busy bar. My tiny heart raced. Only one Community type leaked darkness like that. But what the fuck was a grim reaper doing in Tucson? Was I being rescued? The man I passed was most definitely not Thane.

My lungs seized painfully. Oh gods, did something happen to Thane?

I dove down to the empty street behind the bar and shifted back into my human form between two parked cars. As I raced toward the front door, my pulse thumped in my ears.

"Hold up," barked a gruff voice.

I turned to face the bouncer, a giant of a man I hadn't even noticed in my rush to get inside. I pointed at the open door. "I'm meeting a friend who's already in there."

"Your friend can wait like everyone else." He nodded toward the line of restless bar hoppers glaring at me above the glow of their cell phones.

I eyed the man. Roughly six-foot-two, brown hair, brown eyes, way too much weightlifting. But he was still human, meaning I could take him faster than a Girl Scout could sell cookies outside a grocery store. If I wanted to cause a scene, that is, which I most definitely did not.

Grumbling, I moved to the back of the line. From where I stood and moved steadily closer, I would be able to see anyone coming out. A little bit of tension leaked out of my shoulders, and I sighed. Gods, I missed Miami. There, I knew several club bouncers who would let me straight in thanks to my frequent visits and VIP status. Money really could buy happiness.

Although here in Tucson, no one questioned my lack of club clothes while I stood in line. Pros and cons. At long last, a whopping three minutes later, I was at the front showing my ID to the bouncer. This time he nodded me inside, and I resisted the urge to make a face behind his back. Was this what growing older and wiser at the ripe old age of twenty-seven felt like? I crinkled my nose, not sure I liked the idea of being considered *too old* for this bar.

The music was loud, a steady beat vibrating within my chest, but I barely registered the song as I scanned the crowd. Dim lighting and strobe lights flashing from the dance floor quickly became a distracting nuisance, so I pushed through the random bunches of people, searching for the reaper in the hat and jacket. I wouldn't be able to detect his light repulsing effect while I was in human form, but I still possessed an uncanny ability to sense Community members when I paid attention. Had I done that earlier, I wouldn't be chasing him down to begin with.

The bar wasn't big, which meant my nose was assaulted with the mix of sweat, spilled beer, and way too many clashing perfumes. It also meant that I scoured that place front to back twice in just a handful of minutes. I even convinced a few dudes to check out the men's bathrooms for my "cheating boyfriend." I would have gone in myself, except I'd likely get kicked out. All the emergency exits would set off alarms, and the kitchen staff said no one had gone out the back door.

The reaper was nowhere to be found.

How the fuck did he get away from me again? Did he use his enforcement ability to deflect attention while he snuck out? Was he actively trying to make me go crazy?

If so, consider your job complete, reaper.

I headed back outside through the front door and eyed the darkened streets leading away from the bar. Parked cars only took up half the small lot out front, leaving plenty of wide-open spaces and little room to hide, but there was no sign of the guy.

"Friend bail on you?" asked the bouncer, waving another gaggle of giggling, just turned twenty-one-year-olds inside. I almost longed to be one of them again, without a care in the world and Maddox still alive.

My heart clenched as I imagined my brother's bright green eyes and a smile that lit up any room.

"Something like that," I muttered and walked away, feeling pretty damn defeated.

CHAPTER 3

Tuesday Night

Since I did most of my eating out in the guise of getting to know the town, I didn't have much food at my apartment. I stopped for a few slices of pizza at a place on Broadway. Charlie's Pizzeria was barely large enough to hold three people in line inside but also boasted a walk-up window outside for ordering by the slice. Perfect for late-night munchies, and scouring the skies in falcon form always left me famished.

Carrying a triangle-shaped cardboard box filled with a fresh-out-of-the-oven slice in one hand and a greasy, hot slice of meat lover's pie in the other, I headed for my mini-high rise sharing the same street. A few buildings away from my destination, a scuffle caught my attention down a side street. It was too dark to see anything properly, but the heat signatures told me someone was being jumped by a few others. Selfishly, I decided to keep walking so I could eat in peace; crime rates in Miami and skirmishes during my previous job had numbed me to the shock of witnessing a mugging.

But I nearly choked on my pizza crust when I realized the guy being jumped was *him*—the reaper.

Wait, what? A reaper should be more than capable of handling himself in a fight. They were working their way toward angel wings, for flame's sake, only a notch below holy. Their scythes were made for both reaping and sowing, and they were *very* good at both.

Except, apparently, for this one.

Cursing the poor timing around a mouthful of cheese and pepperoni, I set my box down against a brick wall, hoping it would still be there when I got back. Jogging toward the group, I wiped my hands on my work pants— slippery hands and knives did not go well together. If my slacks were ruined, I'd make these guys buy me a new pair.

I swallowed the last of my food as I approached. Three people pinned the reaper down, securing him with zip ties. Memories of my own recent experience with a zip tie and a nasty game of football against the reanimated dead came flooding back, filling my mouth with a sour taste. Way to ruin a perfectly tasty pizza.

I tilted my head to the side as confusion swept through next. Zip ties shouldn't be enough to keep a reaper down. Had I been wrong after all? Was this just a standard mugging?

Oh well. I could use some exercise and a good deed for karma's sake.

"Hey, kids," I said, drawing my knives from their hidden sheaths. I never left home without my custom blades, complete with fireballs etched down the steel. "Can I play next?"

The two men and a woman holding the possible reaper looked up in a mix of surprise and anger. The men leaped to their feet, a real accomplishment considering the long staffs they held. That was when I realized who I was dealing with: mages.

Why the fuck were mages attacking a reaper?

I threw myself to the side as a spell went whooshing by and collided with a wall. Chunks of concrete and brick went flying, hitting me at the same time as the answer to my question and taking my breath along with it. Damn, a month had made me slow on the uptake. These weren't just mages—they were necromancers.

Was the reaper here to warn me that I'd been found? Gods, I hated having more questions than answers.

I tumbled across the ground to dodge another spell, the side seam of my slacks snagging on the asphalt and ripping. Definitely ruined now.

No longer feeling the need to play nice with people who aligned themselves with pure evil, I hurled a knife at the closest spell-caster. If he liked zombies that much, then he could go become one for all I cared. The blade found its home in his chest, and I was there a moment later to drive it home with a solid kick. He fell to the ground, his hands wrapped around the hilt protruding from his shirt.

I turned to face the other guy right as his fire spell hit

me full on. Flames erupted around my body, lighting me up like a torch. If I had been anyone else, I would've screamed in agony, but a second later the flames fizzled out and became tendrils of smoke fleeing into the night sky.

I couldn't help it—I grinned at the stupidly confused look on the mage's face. You can't fight fire with fire.

"That's the phoenix!" yelled the woman who stayed with a knee on the reaper's back. Why the hell wasn't he fighting her, fighting to get free?

The spell-caster backed away, fear flashing across his face. But I wasn't about to let these jerks go without some answers. I rushed him, ducking under his staff's swing to come up behind him, a blade at his throat. With newfound sparkly spells at their disposal, newer mages hadn't learned the importance of hand-to-hand combat, which worked in my favor. Happy to provide the lesson, I turned him so his friend could see his predicament.

"Why are you in Tucson? And attacking a reaper? Are you after me?" I muttered to myself. "I have so many questions. But first, let him go."

The woman pinning the reaper down looked between me and her friend with eyes the color of an autumn sunset, then smiled. Even with half of it pulled back, long, curly brown hair fell down to the middle of her back. Loose tendrils framed her ivory face, her cheeks flushed from the fight with the reaper. A glamour hid her pointed ears, but I had no problem discerning her true fae nature.

"We're all prepared to die for the cause," she said.

Fuck. She called my bluff. Her friend didn't seem too thrilled about the idea either as he sputtered in response, so I held the knife tighter to his skin to get him to stop squirming. A trickle of blood slid over the blade, and I met the other mage's reddish-brown eyes again. She just smiled and waited.

It was one thing to kill a person who was actively trying to kill you, and a whole other thing to kill someone you held pinned, even an idiot like this one. I sighed. Pulling the knife away, I knocked him hard on the head with the hilt to make sure he went down. The paralyzing poison coated on my blade would keep him that way.

"All right, woman to woman, what the fuck's going on here?"

She chuckled and showed me a dagger she had been hiding in her hand. The weapon was pretty damned fancy, with jewels on the hilt and swirly designs down the blade. That was why the reaper didn't try to escape from beneath her knee? An expensive-looking knife?

I wasn't sure what she wanted me to say. "Neat blade…?"

"Do you know how difficult it is to kill a reaper?" she asked, running a finger down the steel.

My skin crawled with goosebumps. I didn't know precisely, but I'd witnessed Thane and some other reapers fight. I needed to keep her talking until I figured something out. "Not personally, no."

"It's next to impossible, which is why we obtained the Daggers of Abaddon, forged in the Dark Ages by the most powerful necromancers of the time." She moved so the dagger's point was directly above the reaper's heart, through his back.

His eyes met mine in a silent plea.

"Wait, let's think this through." I held up my hands in a show of surrender. "Let me have him, you take your friend, and we all go our own way."

She laughed. "Like I said, phoenix, we're all prepared to die for the cause." She leaned her full weight on the blade, which sank deep into the reaper's back.

As soon as I knew what she intended to do, I sent my blade flying. The steel found its home in the side of her slim neck. She fell back onto the asphalt, grasping at the knife and gurgling as blood spilled out around her.

I rushed to the reaper and sliced through the zip tie, turning him onto his side. Blood soaked the back of his jacket. "Hey, stay with me."

He took a deep, shuddering breath and winced, pointing toward the woman. "My... teleport..."

I leaned over and searched her pockets until I found the cylindrical object. The reaper's hands grabbed for mine, and I pressed the teleportation device into his palm.

"H-help... us..." Gasping, he pushed the button, activating the portal on the ground beside us with his thumbprint. Then he went still, his eyes glazing over in death. The black circle that would whisk us away beckoned, and I only had a matter of moments to make it through before it closed.

I glanced around. The female mage was in her final gurgling stage, twitching as her life force fled. The guy I knocked on the head was still out and paralyzed. I jumped up and grabbed his foot, hauling him closer to the reaper.

This was going to be tough.

I grabbed the reaper's foot in one hand, tucked the mage's leg under my other arm, and stepped onto the black circle.

CHAPTER 4

Tuesday Night

I became semi-accustomed to the feeling of teleporting when I worked with Thane on the Xavier case, but my body apparently forgot the sensation in the past month. All my insides were pulled apart, atom by atom, scrambled around in a blender, then put back together again in the blink of an eye.

It felt as pleasant as it sounded.

The moment the sensation stopped, I put my hands on my knees and bent over, sure I was about to puke. Stomach acid rose, making me dry heave a few times before I could stand straight again. The back of my throat burned.

Adam stared at me from behind his massive mahogany desk, his eyebrows practically lost in his sandy blond hairline.

I opened my mouth to speak but held up a finger instead as another wave of nausea rolled through. When the feeling passed, I tried again. "Reaper is dead, mage is unconscious. Necromancer."

Only then did Adam Larue, the Archangel of Miami and the reaper's boss, seem to register the two men at my feet. He leaped out of his chair, his shimmering white wings spreading out behind him. Yelling some command about needing security out his open door—I was still a bit too dazed to focus on the words—he rushed toward the reaper. Falling to his knees, Adam scooped the man up like he weighed next to nothing and held him to his broad chest, oblivious to the blood. His wings curled around them.

Two more reapers teleported into Adam's office and quickly assessed the scene. They secured the mage with handcuffs, hauling him out of the room as he started to come to. He wasn't one of the fae, so the reapers wouldn't need iron—the human handcuffs would be more than enough to hold him. I hoped they chafed him raw, at least.

Alone with the archangel, I knelt beside him. If it were possible for an angel to look exhausted and disheveled, that would be how I described Adam. It might have been my imagination, but the circles around his eyes appeared darker than usual, dimming his bright blue eyes to a dull navy. His close-cropped blond hair wasn't long enough to be a mess, but something about it seemed off, like it wasn't quite as bright and vibrant as it used to be. Half of his button-down dress shirt was untucked, and I was pretty sure I spied a dirt stain on the side of his tan slacks.

Had he gotten any sleep while I was away? Did angels even need sleep? This one certainly looked like he needed it, and the sooner, the better.

"The woman who killed him was fae," I said quietly. I didn't want to intrude on his grief, but we had work to do now. "She used that blade…she called it one of the Daggers of Abaddon. Does that mean anything to you?"

Adam turned the reaper enough to spot the dagger's jeweled hilt protruding from his back. The archangel let out a deep sigh that was almost a groan. "Unfortunately, yes. A grim reaper can be killed without them, though with much difficulty, but the Daggers act as if the reaper is mortal. One well-placed thrust is all it takes."

He ran a hand over his face before continuing, "The Society of the Dead forged three blades using the fires of hell and an unholy alliance with demons—the Daggers of Abaddon, named in blasphemy for one of God's fiercest destroyers. With the Society's fall at the end of the dark ages, the Daggers were hidden from us. We have searched for centuries. If only we found them first, then Shawn…" He trailed off, grief clouding his eyes.

My blood chilled to ice, and my hands grew clammy against my thighs. Daggers capable of taking down reapers as easily as if they were mortal was a terrifying thought. What if Thane came face to face with one?

Adam carefully laid the reaper on the floor, removing the blade from his back so the body could lay flat. "He was to gain his wings this month."

I swallowed down a lump forming in my throat. No wonder Adam was taking the reaper's death so hard. Not that it wasn't sad all on its own, but angels weren't exactly known for their emotions, more like lack thereof. But gaining a new angel was a big fucking deal. How long had this man worked as a reaper to earn such an achievement?

Reaching out, I took Adam's hand and gave it a squeeze. "I'm so sorry for your loss. With all due respect, I'm going to help you out now whether you want it or not."

"I think I am ready to accept your help." His sad eyes met mine. It was tough to watch such a calm, father-like figure crumble before me. "He is not the first we have lost."

I bit back a curse. "How many?"

"Four, and several more missing." He paused, his gaze traveling over the fallen reaper's form. "They are far stronger than we realized."

"And we will be even stronger," I promised.

A commotion outside the door drew my attention just as another reaper burst into the room. Only it wasn't just any reaper. It was *the* reaper.

Thane.

My body didn't know how to react to the sight. My lungs constricted, my heart leaped into my throat, and my stomach wanted to throw up the pizza—though the last might have been lingering nausea from teleporting. Thane opened his mouth to speak but stopped when he saw me, his beautifully shaped lips still parted in surprise.

"Veronica, what in God's name are you doing here?" he asked.

Dazhbog above, the man was so fucking pretty. Velvety black hair sat in thick waves atop his head, and in this dim office light, his deep blue eyes almost matched it. He had a beautiful caramel hue to his skin, a white boy who spent most of his life outdoors in the sun until he died. His button-down top and slacks mirrored the archangel's, only Thane's were crisply pressed and pristine, and he had an inch or two of height on his boss.

When I opened my mouth to answer his question, all my confused bodily functions caught up with me, and I choked on my godsdamn saliva. As I gasped for air, Thane pulled me to my feet and enveloped me in his muscular arms, holding me to his delightfully hard chest. Heat from his body soothed my cough, and the warmth continued down to my very soul. His lips pressed against the top of my head.

Finally, I felt like I had come home.

Much too soon, he released me and stepped back, taking in the reaper's body on the floor and Adam still kneeling beside him, holding the dagger. "I see," Thane answered his own question that I totally forgot about. His gaze returned to me. "Are you okay?"

"Physically, yes, though I forgot how awful teleporting feels in the beginning." I made a face. "I wish I was returning under happier circumstances."

"Thanks to Ms. Neill's quick thinking, we have one of the mages to question," Adam said, his gaze still glued to the dagger in his hands. He turned it over as he examined the symbols etched down the steel.

Thane smirked in my direction, sending a tingle through my body. I had missed that damn smirk. He twirled a strand of my dyed brown hair around a finger—he didn't see it this color before my escape to the desert. "Not a bad look for you."

"Don't get used to it," I said and turned to Adam. "Why were they in Tucson? Isn't that way too coincidental?"

The archangel rose to his feet, blood from the reaper's

body coating his once pale blue shirt. His usually pristine white feathers looked as though he had dipped them in red paint. "I learned a group of mages was heading west and sent Shawn to keep an eye on them should they get too close."

"Why the hell didn't he call you once they made it to Tucson?" I asked.

The shadows darkened beneath his eyes. This man had seen some long days. "We lost communication a day ago. I assumed he was taken along with some of the others and readied a team to search for him. I will need to extract his memories to be certain."

That sounded morbid. "Extract as in phone a necromancer?"

"Memory retrieval does not take quite as much skill or magic as performing a Rising. But we always have one capable of both on staff."

I shuddered. A necromantic mage was nearby this whole time, and I didn't have a clue. Maybe it was Dr. Owen Cooper, the mortician whose hand I shook while he wasn't wearing gloves. Yuck. "I understand warfare and all that, but why are they taking the reapers and not just outright killing them? Is William that into torture?"

Adam and Thane exchanged a glance I definitely didn't like. It was Thane who spoke. "They're trying to siphon our magic for use in spells, and when that doesn't succeed, they're attempting to turn us into Risen."

The living flame inside me shrank down as if to hide, creating a sense of terror that froze my limbs. Holy fuck. Just when I thought William couldn't get any worse, he went and pulled this shit. "Would reapers be able to use their abilities once they Rise, like the shifters?" I asked, my voice catching at the end.

"We don't know yet." Adam moved behind his mahogany desk, shoving papers and pens out of the way and carefully laying down the dagger. He picked up his desk phone and addressed his secretary.

Yet. What a terrifying thought, one I hoped we would never find out for sure. I turned to Thane, eagerly drinking in the sharp angles and planes of his face. "Can you let Kit know I'm back? I left everything in Tucson, phone included."

Without hesitation, he pulled out his cell phone and shot off a message. After tucking his phone away again, his eyes met mine. He took my hand, pulling me closer. "I missed you."

My heart thumped harder. "Not enough danger in your life without me?"

He smirked and leaned his head closer to mine, his gaze dipping to my lips. "Not enough fire. You must have taken the heat with you."

"Only if you mean a dry heat." I licked my suddenly parched lips, very aware of his gaze tracking the movement.

A wicked gleam twinkled in his eyes. "You prefer being wet?"

"Adam?" A familiar voice spoke from the open doorway, followed by a quick knock on the frame.

I whipped around to glare at the fae who had wined, dined, then betrayed me.

Colin.

CHAPTER 5

Tuesday Night

When Colin recognized me through my dyed hair and fake brown contacts, his mouth slowly dropped open, which would have been comical in any other situation. His brown hair sparkled with red streaks in the office light—natural highlights—and his blue-green eyes met mine, shifting colors as easily as the ocean. The fae man always looked glamorous. He was just as tall as Thane but of a slimmer build. More sturdy palm tree than thick oak, and a whole lot less tan.

"Aren't you supposed to be in Tucson?" he asked, his tone genuinely surprised.

I narrowed my eyes. "You've got a lot of nerve asking

me a stupid question like that the first time you see me after what went down at the stadium."

He winced at the reminder of the situation where I thought he betrayed me by working with William, the fae necromancer responsible for this whole mess. Not to mention it was the event that made me reveal myself as a phoenix to those in attendance to save myself and Thane.

And just what happened next?

Oh yeah, William told *everyone* in the Community what I really was and put a fucking bounty on my head. As the highest-ranking Community enforcement official in Miami, Adam had called for a cease and desist on the bounty, but did that actually work? Of course not. Once a greedy motherfucker, always a greedy motherfucker.

Hence my trip to Tucson.

Colin's eyebrows drew together. "I thought Adam told you I was working for him."

"Oh yes, *Adam* did."

He sighed. "Veronica, I'm terribly sorry for having to keep my work from you."

I supposed that was a start. I didn't actually know what I wanted from him, but I hated knowing the guy was a double agent the whole time, and I didn't have the foggiest idea. Did he have to tell me? Of course not. We hardly knew each other, but it still felt shady somehow, like I had been used to further his purpose. So what if that purpose turned out to be a good one?

Time to start letting my hurt pride go. I gave him a quick nod of acknowledgment. "Does William know the truth about you yet?"

"No, he still believes I work solely for him. I was the

one who created the few Risen found wandering loose. It was necessary to hide my involvement while also providing Adam with information." He paused, his gaze taking in how close together Thane and I stood. "But what are you doing here?"

I explained what happened with the reaper and the mages back in the desert, finishing up just when Adam hung up the phone.

"How has the Society come back to life so quickly and with such numbers?" I asked.

"It may seem that way here in the human realm," Colin said, "but William has been working for decades in the Otherworld, convincing those who think like him that the time has come for the queen and the Summer Court to step down. That the Winter Court should rule once again. He's set up an academy at his home in the mountains, where he trains interested fae in shadow magic…including the art of necromancy."

The mere thought of a Winterlands house in the mountains sent a shiver up my spine. Cold and phoenixes did *not* mix. "I don't understand why he's using the dead to do it. And how the hell did he even get into this realm? The unseelie shouldn't be able to cross through."

Colin's face darkened. "William has been luring other fae to his side with promises of grandeur. Through their studies of the shadow arts, likely using a Summer Court victim, he discovered the unfortunate side effect of Raising a Community member, and the idea grew from there." He let out a deep sigh. "As to your other question, I've made the assumption he has a realm walker working for him, but I have yet to confirm that theory."

My skin prickled as the tiny hairs on my arms and back of my neck rose. Realm walkers were a rare commodity, but their magic allowed them to pass through any dimensional barrier without hesitation, no portals needed. The magic that kept unseelie from crossing over from the Otherworld only worked with already-existing portals; a realm walker would have no issue bringing an unseelie into the human world, except for the fact that it was a taboo and highly illegal practice. Not that an illegal name tag kept anyone from doing anything these days.

I hadn't known about realm walkers at all until recently, and I only knew this much now because Jackson Reed, the man who killed my brother Maddox, was one. He would still be realm walking, except his new iron chains courtesy of the maximum-security supernatural prison kept him from using his magic. My genius best friend helped me get into the prison against Adam's orders to face Jackson, not that it did me much good except present more questions about my past.

Most important being: why the fuck did someone pay Jackson to kill off the last of the phoenixes?

"Has William mentioned the Daggers of Abaddon?" Adam picked up the dagger and handed it to Colin, who turned it over in his hands, inspecting it.

"No, that's news to me, which could mean he's becoming suspicious of my loyalty. He's not the most trusting individual to begin with." Colin brought the Dagger to his nose and sniffed the length of it, which was just weird to watch. To each their own.

The archangel nodded. "And Queen Fiadh, is she aware of William's activities?"

Colin pulled the blade away from his face and scowled. "The queen has yet to grant a private audience. I can't provide her with context without the potential of tipping off William's spies."

"What about Prince Edric?" I asked. "Didn't you say you were here on his behalf?"

"I have reason to believe he may be involved with William." Colin pressed his lips together firmly and returned the Dagger to Adam.

Interesting. I didn't know the prince, but he had waltzed in on Thane and me when we checked out Duke Broderick Ó Faoláin's home. A Master Vampire named Xavier had murdered the duke to help a grim reaper cheat her way to wings and thought he would get me as a prize. Nope. Anyway, the prince didn't know I was in the duke's house snooping around. Back then, I was sure Edric had something to do with the box and soul theft. He didn't, but now even Colin was suspicious of the prince's shady behavior.

"I will send Nathan with you to the Otherworld," Adam said. "The queen needs to be made aware of what her subjects are doing here, although I fear it will only fuel her cause."

"Do you think she already knows?" I asked. It had become common knowledge that the queen wanted all fae to return to the Otherworld. As in forever.

Adam and Colin exchanged a thoughtful glance. Colin spoke first, "It's possible. But why she's not outright condemning him and his followers isn't something I can answer."

"She would not turn down a private audience with an

angel," Adam added. "Nathan will make sure she is aware and takes swift action. Unless…" He glanced at Thane. "I would like you to accompany Nathan to the Otherworld."

Thane's eyebrows pulled together. "Sir?"

"You experienced firsthand the horrors and atrocities being committed against the human realm as well as Community members. You saw her own kind performing these rituals. It would be a far stronger message coming from you."

"If he goes, I go," I blurted out. Dazhbog's light, me and my big mouth just couldn't quit.

Adam turned an amused smile on me. "I am glad to see you are agreeable. I planned to ask you as well, since you also witnessed the fae necromancers and may be able to identify them for her."

"Oh, right. Smart." I knew without looking that Thane was smirking in my direction. That smug bastard.

"Colin will escort the three of you through the portal tomorrow," Adam said.

My nostrils flared. I understood Colin wasn't actually the bad guy here, but I was still having a hard time coming to terms with the fact that he had been hiding such a huge secret from me. I know, I know, he was undercover, but logic didn't prevail over my hurt feelings just yet. I really started to think of the guy as a potential suitor until I saw him standing beside William in the stadium. My stomach lurched at the memory.

"With all due respect, Adam," Thane said, "we should leave right away. Today. The longer we wait, the more opportunity William has to gain the upper hand."

The angel nodded. "I understand, but first I need Ms.

Neill to speak with Luka Navarro."

I blinked. Why in the world did he want me to meet with the resident alpha werewolf? "Why me?"

"I believe he is fonder of you than you realize for the service you provided to his betrothed." Adam smiled. "I am calling on all the Community leaders to assist in this matter. We need his wolves to help track down the Risen and their creators."

My heart swelled with pride and happiness, and a grin spread across my face. Luka and Tabitha were engaged! A week of courtship might seem fast to most people, but they were in love for years and knew each other better than most couples just starting out. They lost enough time together; no sense in waiting. I couldn't have asked for a better outcome with the whole trying to steal a ring and almost getting myself killed by the alpha incident.

"Look at what the cat dragged in," drawled a voice at the door that I would recognize anywhere.

I might have shattered some eardrums with my squeal as I ran over to envelop my best friend in a tight squeeze. As expected, Kit's body stiffened beneath my attack before softening enough to hug me back. She wasn't exactly a hugger, but she would make an attempt for me. That was love.

"You better not have blood on you," she said when I finally let her go and stepped back.

Through a blur of watery eyes, I noted the light mascara, the soft pink blush across her cedar brown skin. She was wearing makeup? On a Tuesday? Her braids were pulled back into a half ponytail, which helped reveal the newest image shaved onto one half of her head—a lightning bolt.

Her t-shirt displayed a dragon hoarding a pile of books, and for the first time ever, her jeans didn't sport a single rip or fray. Even her toenails were painted, poking out the top of her Birkenstock sandals.

I looked down at my clothes, suddenly self-conscious. I had hugged Thane, too. Or rather, he hugged me while I choked on my spit, and I returned the squeeze. Luckily, no major stains made themselves known.

Kit cleared her throat. Only then did I realize she hadn't come alone.

"V, this is Angela," Kit said, her cheeks dimpling slightly with a smile.

I pushed strands of my dark brown hair behind my ear before reaching out to shake the newcomer's hand. Her skin was like a glass of pure milk, not an ounce of espresso to be found. The top of her head barely reached my chin, and her hair was as dark as mine dyed, only made up of tight, ringlet curls. Milk chocolate-colored eyes gazed into mine with genuine warmth. The slightest tingle of magic crossed between our hands. She might not have been a natural-born witch like Kit, but she certainly wasn't helpless. Even if she looked like she would fit in my pocket.

"It's so nice to finally meet you." Her voice held a sing-song quality, and her pale pink lips held a warm smile.

I was utterly unprepared for this petite woman to be Angela. She was so delicate and so unlike any woman Kit dated in the past, and I wasn't sure yet if that was a good or bad thing. Likely good, as those women often turned out to be power-hungry, greedy, or lazy as fuck. I was certain Kit nursed a savior complex somewhere deep inside. Maybe that was why she had befriended me so easily.

"Same, and I take it Kit has come clean about our world." I grinned at my best friend, knowing that it was a big step for her.

Angela's gaze flicked to Adam and his shimmering white wings. "Yes. It has been…very eye-opening."

"You just can't stay out of trouble, can you?" Kit asked.

"Hey, trouble found me this time." I put my hands up in defense.

As the conversation turned back to our trip to the Otherworld, I realized that Kit didn't introduce Angela to anyone else, which meant she had already met everyone here. I knew Kit agreed to work alongside Thane in my place while I was gone, but I didn't know Angela would be doing the same. Or at the very least meeting Community leaders as high up as Adam. And a double agent?

My stomach clenched and burned. I was jealous. Totally jealous that I was the last to meet my best friend's girlfriend, that even *Colin* had gotten the chance to meet her. I missed out on something so important because of a stupid fae who learned to Raise the dead, all in the name of throwing an epic temper tantrum.

I clenched my teeth together. Ognebog help me, I wanted to kill that bastard William even more now.

CHAPTER 6

Wednesday Morning

Thane coughed, a slightly embarrassed sound, as if it would somehow get me to stop what I was doing. "It's just a car, Veronica."

I turned my head to glare at him, but I refused to stand just yet. I had all but thrown myself across the hood of my bright red Mercedes Benz Maybach convertible when we met in the garage that morning. I'd waxed and covered her before I headed for the desert, so she was just as shiny as when I left, which was also good because it meant my white linen shorts and black top weren't covered in dirt. I was sure the wolves wouldn't mind, but I sure did.

My car was the closest thing I had to a baby, and I'd

missed my girl. The purr of her idle and the roar of her engine were as dear to me as a newborn's coos and a toddler's laughs. If I wanted to lay across her hood with my sandals barely brushing the cement below and my arms spread eagle to grip either side, then no amount of judgment from a reaper would stop me.

"Don't interrupt my reunion." Yes, this might've been the most ridiculous reaction for a grown woman to have—like, ever—but having to abruptly leave my whole life behind in the blink of an eye really did a number on me. I might not hide my purple irises behind brown contacts anymore, but brown dye still tinted my beautiful white-blonde hair, for fuck's sake. I would hug my damn car if I wanted to.

Thane rolled his eyes and climbed in the passenger side. I gave myself another moment to enjoy my nearly-returned-to-normal life, then slid to the ground. No one but me drove the Benz, so I started her up and gave her engine a few revs. She roared like a tigress on the prowl—shifter and pure animal alike. Smiling, I eased her out of the garage and onto the busy Miami streets, heading for the alpha werewolf's house on the outskirts of the city.

After we wrapped up our discussion in Adam's office the night before, Kit and Angela returned to my best friend's place, planning to stay as far away from this mess as possible now that I returned. I was relieved knowing I wouldn't have to worry about them, but I also really wanted to get to know Angela. That time would come but try telling that to my patience.

Adam insisted on having two angels accompany me back to my penthouse apartment, which was still a secret to the rest of the Community. William hadn't been able to ruin that for me. It would be a safe place for the time being.

My sweeter-than-cotton candy guardian angel, Jessa, restocked my fridge and cookie jar before I got there. She left me the cutest note—complete with hearts dotting the i's—about how sorry she was that she couldn't stay to welcome me home in person. I could have kissed her for her foresight. I hadn't flown home, an act that required intense amounts of energy and resulted in food binges, ravenous hunger threatening to eat me from the inside out, but I was still pretty damn hungry from the night's events. Also, I never got to finish my pizza.

Oh, Miami, how I missed you. It was like the gods wanted to welcome me home with a gorgeous, crystal clear blue sky, the sun climbing its way up and warming the earth. Buildings rose high into the sky, reaching for the clouds and actually touching them on some low ceiling days. A crisp, salty sea breeze swept around the towers and through our open car windows. It teased my hair into flight and brought with it traditional Cuban dance beats from the open windows of a mom-and-pop restaurant. No matter how interesting Tucson was and how I'd grown to appreciate its unique beauty, this was the city I was meant to be in.

Thane somehow sensed my need to soak in the city, staying quiet on the drive over to Luka's. That or he was waiting for me to say something, but I was too busy sighing in happiness every few minutes. Good things always seemed to come to an end much too soon.

"Sounds like you guys have been busy since I left," I said, finally feeling recharged.

He leaned an arm against the door. "Non-stop action. We could have used another explosion like at the stadium."

"Yeah, well, that's what you all get for sending me away."

"Someone has to keep you safe." He grinned as I threw a glare his way. "Tell me about Tucson."

I shrugged. "Not a whole lot to tell. It's hot, dry, and far from everything I love." My heart fluttered. "What do you think about Angela?"

He glanced my way with a knowing look. "You jealous?"

I scoffed. Oh, who was I kidding? "Just that I'm the last to meet her."

"She's pretty chill. You'll like her."

Strands of my hair flew in front of my face with the breeze. "How would you know what I like?"

"I know you better than you think. You're not as mysterious as you try to be."

"How dare you," I said with as much indignation I could muster without laughing. "I am all kinds of mystery."

"Not to me." His words were soft and full of emotion.

My heart was going to beat right out of my chest with that level of sweetness. At least his kind of sweet wouldn't make my teeth rot.

Gravel crunched beneath the tires as I pulled off the main street and onto Luka's long driveway. Perfect timing for a distraction. This far out from downtown, the road wound through the thick green foliage and overhanging trees before dropping us in front of a block on stilts. There really was no other way to describe the alpha's house. It was a small building, probably only made up of two or three tiny bedrooms and maybe one or two equally tiny bathrooms. I wasn't judging, I just expected a bit more opulence for a wolf pack leader.

But then, I knew from my past research that he spent a decent amount of time outside and in the woods. Maybe they even kept an actual wolf den somewhere. What happened in the pack generally stayed in the pack. I was lucky to know the little that I did thanks to Tabitha, the alpha's mate. She had hired me to get her deceased husband's ring back.

The only problem? Luka, as in the alpha wolf, had the band, and he wasn't too keen on giving it up. The ring belonged to the pack, and Tabitha had left the pack after Luka killed her father, the previous alpha.

Sad, right?

It turned out that her father had gone berserk, and Luka was saving his pack—and Tabitha's life—by challenging him. Anyway, the good news is I ignored Jessa's request to stay put after the stadium explosion, played matchmaker, and now everyone was happy.

The front door opened as we climbed out of the Benz, and a little boy with soaking-wet dark brown hair ran down the front steps, aiming straight for me. I recognized him as Tabitha's cub, no more than three years old. He skidded to a stop right in front of me and gazed up into my face with the honey-colored eyes he shared with his mother. A floral scent drifted off of him.

"I know you," he said matter-of-factly, then he was off, heading behind the house just as Tabitha came running out the front door, the front of her yellow tank top speckled with water. He would be safe; there were plenty of wolves around to keep an eye on him.

"Julian!" Her exasperated tone spoke volumes. She caught sight of me, her expression going through confusion and shock before settling on joy. "Veronica, what in the full moon's pull are you doing here? And what the hell did you do to your hair?"

She came down the few front steps, and we hugged. I smiled at the change to her own appearance: she was in clean, unwrinkled clothes, no exhaustion weighing her down like when we first met. She wore her thick brown hair in a long braid down her back, just sweeping the top of her butt. Her eyes sparkled as she looked at me in a similarly appraising light, which changed to a sly glance shot toward Thane.

"Tabitha, this is Agent Thane Munro of the DEA," I said. "As much as I'd love to catch up, we're here on behalf of the agency. Is Luka around?"

Her expression changed to one of apprehension. "Of course. Please come in."

"Nothing bad, I promise." I gave a rueful smile. "Well, not for the wolves, anyway."

"Mind the wet footprints." She waved a hand at puddles on the floor as we followed her inside the house to the living room. "I just finished giving Julian a bath, which means he's out getting dirty again."

After she pulled away a sheet lying across the two-seater couch, she motioned for us to sit. When you can come and go as a wolf, hair tends to get everywhere. A sheet is far easier to throw in the wash than a couch.

I had no idea where we were on the lunar calendar, but it didn't matter the way you'd think it would when it came to werewolves—they could shift any day of the month. Sure, their prowess was at peak performance on full moons, but they were fierce predators no matter the time or day. Supernaturally enhanced strength and speed and all that jazz. I was glad to have them on our side and not William's.

"Something to drink?" she asked. "Iced tea? Water?"

"Tea would be lovely." I wasn't thirsty, but my mother raised me to let a hostess host.

"Lemon?"

"No, thank you."

She didn't wait for Thane to reply before leaving us to settle ourselves on the worn yet still comfy couch, which wasn't her being rude, seeing how reapers didn't eat or drink anything. A moment later, she popped back in with a glass of iced tea, Luka at her heels.

Even though the man had a shirt on this time and was betrothed to the woman beside him, I couldn't stop the drool accumulating in my mouth. Sun above, he was delightful to look at. Thick, wavy black hair tempted anyone to run their fingers through, while dark amber eyes gazed straight into your soul. As he leaned forward with a hand out, the muscles beneath his rich russet skin undulated, adding to his overall attraction.

Damn, Tabitha was a lucky lady.

"Ms. Neill, Mr. Munro," he said in his thick Spanish accent, shaking our hands. Because good looks weren't enough for this alpha, he had to have a sexy accent, too. "I appreciate you not coming in through my window this time." He grunted when Tabitha elbowed him in the side.

"Yeah, well, Thane isn't as sneaky as I am." I grinned back at the wolf's wink.

"Some of us have no need to sneak in and out of places," Thane said, equal parts humor and exasperation tinting his tone.

"Right, because you can teleport," I pointed out.

"You all chat. I've got things to do around here, like find one very precocious cub." Tabitha waved and left, and Luka sat in the only other chair in the tiny living room.

"To what do I owe the pleasure of your visit?" he asked, leaning back in the chair.

"The Archangel of Miami requests the pack's assistance tracking down the location of the Society of the Dead," Thane said.

He sure didn't skirt around the issue. While considering Thane's words, the alpha rubbed his cleanly shaven chin. Unlike reapers and vampires, werewolves grew facial hair and the hair on top of their heads at obscenely fast rates, especially around a full moon. Chances were he would have to shave again today—maybe even more than once—to keep the bare chin look. Although, I was absolutely certain he would look even more tempting with a beard. Ruggedly handsome wasn't always my thing, but on some men…

"This must be a serious issue for Adam to come to us," he said.

"It is dire. The mages are going after and successfully capturing and murdering reapers." Thane allowed that to sink in for a moment. When Luka's mouth dropped open, the reaper continued, "Adam is calling on all the leaders of the Community to help stop this menace before it gets out of hand."

I managed to stop my eye roll. The situation was already way out of hand, but who was I to correct the reaper?

"How has the Society survived all these years?" Luka asked.

"The man calling himself their leader is a fae of the Winter Court," Thane explained. "William Caomhánach."

Luka's head snapped back. "An unseelie? Here? How is that possible?"

"We believe he has a realm walker on his staff," the reaper explained. "But even worse, fae magic has had some unexpected consequences with the Risen. Not only can they Raise Community members, but the shifters also maintain their ability in death."

If I thought Luka was shocked before, I didn't have a word for his face now. His brown skin paled as the blood drained from his face, and he ran a shaking hand through his hair. Not that I would ever call him out for being scared—the feeling was warranted and mutual. That was just how bad the situation had gotten.

"We will help the agency, of course," Luka said at last, leaning forward to rest his elbows on his knees. "Just tell me what you need us to do."

Thane discussed logistics with the alpha wolf, which included tracking the Risen mobs' origins and the mages' locations from the last places reapers and other Community members were attacked. The wolves were given the all-clear to destroy any Risen they found and asked to call the DEA for cleanup purposes. The Community was still hidden from the human world, and we were trying desperately to keep it that way.

After that, Luka walked us to the door, where Tabitha met us, removing dirt-stained gloves.

"We'll do our best, searching day and night," Luka said,

his expression stern.

Thane extended a hand, and they shook again. "I have no doubt."

Tabitha pulled me in for a hug, the smell of a warm hearth drifting from her. "Let's plan a get together after this is all over, hm?"

The smile that filled my face was as genuine as they got. "I'd love to."

Sweet Mokosh, did I finally make another friend?

CHAPTER 7

Wednesday Morning

Thane and I left the wolves to plan their search while we headed back into the heart of Miami. Only a few minutes into the drive, he reached across and captured my hand, and I nearly jumped out of my seat from the shock that rushed through my body. It was electric, filling me with warmth and desire and comfort all at once.

I allowed him to slide his fingers between mine until he held my hand in his strong grip, the roughened skin of his palm lightly brushing mine. My insides skipped and danced as he raised our joined hands to his lips and kissed my knuckles. Thank the sun above that he had chosen a moment at a stoplight, because I likely would have crashed the car with that kiss. My body was molten, on fire in the best and worst way. When the light turned green, he set my hand back on the center armrest but didn't let go. I swallowed hard against my suddenly dry mouth.

"I've been meaning to ask you," I said slowly, "but do you feel a certain, uh, not normal way when we touch?"

He laughed. "Not normal? Is that how you feel?"

"I mean, it's intense." I glanced at him out of the corner of my eye, catching his sobering look. "You set me on fire, and considering what I am, that's not normal."

"I—" He turned to look at me, his eyes flying wide. "Veronica, look out!"

A sharp pain split through my skull, and I rolled to my side, my ears ringing. Grass scratched at my cheek and arms, and I caught the scent of something burning. Rubber? I opened my eyes, squinting against the intense light of the sun. Through blurred vision, I faced the crumpled driver's side door of my Benz, only from the side of the road. The window was shattered, shards of glass littering the ground around me.

Sun and flames, what happened? The car was a tangled mess of metal and smoke, though no fire had broken out yet. I took inventory of my body without moving, noting the bruises and strains but not identifying anything worse. How the hell was I outside the car? Had I died and resurrected?

My vision cleared and adjusted to the light, revealing a cloaked figure crouched on the vehicle's hood, peering inside the fractured windshield.

"Hey!" I tried to yell, but only a croak came out.

The figure snapped its head toward me. Dark shadows formed beneath a deep hood, keeping the face hidden except for glowing yellow eyes that looked vaguely familiar. Paranoia prickled down my spine. Where had I seen those eyes before?

Tires squealed to a stop, drawing my attention away. Humans exited the new car in a rush, running over to ours.

When I looked back, the figure on the hood of my car was gone. Damn it. What the fuck did he do to us?

"Are you okay?" a grey-haired woman asked as she knelt by my side, helping me sit up.

I put a hand to my head, which spun for a moment before righting itself. "Yeah, just dazed. Is my friend still in the car?"

"My husband is getting him out now." Behind the woman, the passenger door groaned open, and a man leaned inside to check on Thane.

"Did you see someone on the hood just now? A guy, or maybe a girl, with a cloak and glowing eyes?" I asked, glancing around us. A bent and twisted bumper hung loosely from the front of a pickup truck not too far away from the Benz. The cause of the accident because I sure as shit didn't run a stop sign.

"Oh, dear." The woman put her hands on my shoulders to keep me from rising. "You've got a concussion. Stay right here. The ambulance is on its way."

I did as I was told, but not necessarily because I needed an ambulance. I checked out my arms and legs, expecting to see cuts and scrapes or worse, but finding none. Just dirt and grass stains, which meant these white shorts were ruined. Even a few spots of blood—but no wounds. I might have healed fast as a phoenix, but I didn't heal *this* fast.

Thane knelt beside me, blood dripping down a gash on his forehead, though it was already congealing as it healed. "Are you hurt?"

The woman who helped me patted my shoulder and hurried over to help her husband with the occupant of the other vehicle.

I let out a small laugh. "You're the one bleeding."

"Seriously, Veronica." His eyes scanned over my body, assessing me. Confusion drew his eyebrows together. "You're not hurt."

"Don't sound so bummed." I took his hand and stood, only swaying slightly as my legs quivered. "Someone was here."

I opened my mouth to tell him about the shadowy figure, who I now suspected had pulled me out of the car and might have healed me somehow, but a scream split the air. My gaze snapped toward the other vehicle, where a man missing half his face leaned out of the broken driver's side window and gnawed on the elderly woman's arm—a Risen. She shrieked as her husband tried to pull her away.

Thane and I sprinted over. I snatched a knife from a hidden sheath tucked into my waistband and forced it through the Risen's paper thin cheek with a little help from my inner fire. The blade's flat side slid between his teeth until I turned it, forcing the jaws open like a crowbar.

Freed from the dead man's hold, the woman and man collapsed and scooted backward. Their eyes were round saucers as Thane dispatched the Risen by forcing its forehead onto broken glass still attached to the door. The body stopped wriggling.

The good news was the woman wouldn't have to worry about turning into a Risen from the bite—only a necromancer could do that—but she'd need to wash it to avoid infection. Dead mouths were nasty places.

Thane waved me over and pointed inside. The Risen's remaining foot bones were strapped to the gas pedal and the steering wheel locked into place.

"Holy shit, how did anyone know we'd be out here?" I asked.

Something else didn't sit quite right. Why the hell had someone simply sent some Risen to hit our car? Our attacker had to be close enough to—

A low growl came from the top of the truck, where a black panther glared down at me, hunger in his yellow eyes. A shifter.

As soon as the realization struck, the big cat leaped for me. I spun out of the way, but my arm burned as sharp claws raked across my skin. A second later, I had two knives in my hands, circling the cat. In my periphery, Thane grappled with three masked figures, but the panther leaped again before I could determine if he needed my help. I took on the full blow this time, holding his teeth at bay as we fell backward onto the grass. He would have expected me to dodge again, which meant he didn't expect my knife in his side.

I slipped the blade between his ribs as we rolled. He let out an ear-piercing yowl, but I didn't let him jump away. I ended up holding him down between my legs.

"Who are you?" I twisted the blade. "Why are you attacking us?"

Yellow cat eyes glared back at me, but he didn't revert to human form. Only some shifters could speak while in their animal forms, like Luka as a wolf. I definitely couldn't with a beak for a mouth.

The cat's tongue rolled out as he panted, then his eyes went wide. Shimmering beneath my hold, his body shifted into human form. Thankfully fully dressed, considering how I straddled his hips. "We were right." His chuckle turned to a gargle as the movement drove my knife deeper between his ribs.

"Right about what?"

"I thought we'd been tricked, that this car was a decoy," he said, his voice failing. "But you're her. The phoenix."

Ah. The hair dye likely fooled these idiots until this one got close enough to sniff me out. I glared at him. "You hoped to collect that traitor's bounty?"

He drew a rasping breath, blood starting to pool in his mouth. I must have punctured a lung. Killing him wasn't my intention, but I was fucking pissed. They destroyed my baby and tried to capture me.

"We all gotta eat, right?" He released his breath, and his eyes glazed over in death.

I muttered and pulled my knife free. There were other ways to earn enough of a living to feed yourself. I learned that lesson, too, but I didn't turn to kidnapping people for a bounty. Stealing goods might not have been exactly moral, but it was higher on the morality scale than this. Robin Hood would agree with me.

Remembering the other bounty hunters attacking Thane, I jumped to my feet.

The masked cowards were fleeing into the surrounding trees, and the reaper approached the couple who had stopped to help us. He crouched in front of the man and woman. Their mouths hung open in shock after witnessing the attack, and the woman held her bitten and bloody arm, tears streaming down her face. At least she wasn't screaming anymore.

Thane said something to them too quietly for me to hear, but both the humans' eyes glossed over, memories erased. Witches and warlocks typically did the erasing so that reapers could keep on reaping, but these were desperate times. He stood and took my hand, pulling out his teleportation device. As the holographic circle appeared, ready to whisk us away, I glanced back at my beautiful car, crushed into an unrecognizable hunk of metal. Tears pricked the corners of my eyes.

It might have been another silly reaction to have over a car, but my heart ached at the thought of losing her. She had been with me through most of my trials and tribulations over the last three years, through so much heartache.

There would be no bringing her back. No necromancy existed for cars.

"Grab the Risen's hand," Thane said.

I snapped my attention back to him. "Ew. What?"

"We need to take it with us, but I need to hang on to you and this device." He waved the teleportation device for emphasis.

With a grimace, I did as told, cringing at the unnaturally dry, bony hand beneath mine. I refused to look, knowing I would definitely throw up if I did. Thane drew us into the black circle, and every bit of me threatened to pull itself apart before sewing itself back together. Solid ground beneath my feet let me know we were in Adam's office.

I dropped the dead hand and jumped away as the body

flopped to the ground.

When Adam walked through the door and saw the Risen and us, he sighed and called out over his shoulder, "I need another cleanup crew in my office."

CHAPTER 8

Wednesday Afternoon

We let Adam know that bounty hunters were still trying to collect William's bounty despite the archangel's cease and desist, and now some of them knew about my disguise thanks to the few who got away from Thane. No blame to him.

After the update, the angel sent us off to shower and change. He thought it wouldn't be proper to appear before the fae queen in blood and grass-stained clothes and smelling like the dead. I disagreed—showing her exactly what we were up against could help our case. But I didn't argue too hard; the inside of my nose burned from my own stench.

The only good thing to come of the bounty hunter

encounter was finding out they still expected me to be blonde, and the brunette threw them off my scent, so to speak. We had no idea how fast the word would spread, or if our attackers would keep it a secret from any other hunters. They hadn't struck me as geniuses, so time would tell if they played it smart or decided to brag about how close they'd gotten.

Thane had paperwork to fill out after the crash, so I used the limited free time after my shower to pop over to Kit's. My best friend hadn't answered my texts over the last hour, which sent a shiver of apprehension up my spine. She *always* responded. The last message I got said she was heading home after lunch with Angela.

I let myself into her apartment with the key she'd given me years ago, bracing myself for a scene of death and destruction. The one-bedroom's open-concept layout let me see from the kitchen to the living room without any walls getting in the way. The place was as immaculate as ever. Except, it was also different. I furrowed my eyebrows as I stepped farther in, eyeing a new pink throw blanket over the back of the couch and some never-before-seen knickknacks and gadgets on the kitchen counter. Had Kit moved?

The bathroom door opened on my right, and I jumped back a step. Laughing, Angela walked out, using a towel to dry her curly, dark brown hair. Kit was hot on her heels. When Angela finally saw me, she screamed and dropped the towel. At least she was dressed already. Kit stepped in front of her girlfriend, fists up and ready for a fight.

I raised my hands in surrender.

"V?" Kit frowned and dropped her arms. The brown skin showing on her chest above her top glistened as water dripped from her multitude of braids. "You've never used the key before."

"Guilty. But you weren't answering my texts."

"We were kind of busy." She gave me a pointed look.

I put my hands on my hips. "Yeah, me too, getting into a car crash thanks to some bounty hunters who tracked me down. I wanted to make sure you were safe."

Her expression softened, but it was Angela who asked, "Oh, Veronica, are you okay?" She rushed forward to envelop me in a hug.

I blinked a few times before I thought to return the gesture. When she pulled away to look me over, I said, "Yes, and I'm glad to see you guys are, too." I threw Kit an equally pointed look over the top of Angela's head.

Kit rolled her eyes and walked past me to the kitchen. "Well, now that you're here, I've got news for you, too. But do you need anything to eat?"

"No, I drove. Adam's got a reaper bodyguard following me around."

"Thane? Did you leave him outside?"

I grinned, wishing I'd had the foresight to do just that. "No, he's moved on to paperwork hell. What's the news?"

Angela joined Kit in the kitchen, and they wrapped their arms around each other. "Angela moved in a couple of weeks ago."

There was nothing I could do to stop it—my mouth dropped open. They had only been dating, what? Two months max? And moving in a few weeks ago meant after a month, if that.

"I can tell what you're thinking." Kit smirked. "And yes, I know it seems early. But when you've lived this long, and dated as much as I have, you know when you've found the right one. Angela is it for me." She turned a loving smile on her girlfriend. "My fated mate, if such a thing existed for witches."

Angela smiled back and lifted on her tiptoes to give Kit a kiss. "Soulmates."

My thoughts were doing all kinds of gymnastics. On the one hand, I was beyond happy for my best friend. Finding someone she wanted to spend her life with was huge. Like, it had taken a century kind of huge. But on the other hand, it was so fucking *fast*. I didn't know much about Angela yet, and my spidey senses were on hyper-alert with everything else going on.

If Kit trusted her, then I guess so would I. And if Angela did anything to hurt my best friend? Well, I killed when I needed to.

"Wow," I finally said and smiled. Genuine happiness won out. "Definitely not what I expected, but who am I to judge?"

"What did you expect me to say, that I was pregnant?"

"I know you've got maternal instincts buried deep down inside there somewhere."

Kit muttered something under her breath, but Angela laughed. "Closer than you think. I tried to resist her attempts to teach me more about earth magic, but she can be very persuasive."

I raised my eyebrows at Kit. Pushing someone to learn magic was highly unusual for someone who stopped using it herself.

"I want her to be protected if I'm not around." Kit shrugged. "I don't have to use it myself to teach it, and earth is the easiest element to tap into."

That was true. Witches and warlocks attuned themselves to one or two of the four primary elements: earth, fire, air, and water. From our previous discussions, I knew Kit had mastered fire and earth, speaking to how powerful a witch she was before giving up magic. Rarely did a witch attune to more than two due to the tremendous strain on their magical reservoirs and bodies.

Even more rare was a witch also attuned to the fifth element—the soul—an achievement that required mastery over all four primary elements as well. Kit told me that no such witch or warlock existed in centuries, and the Community had started to wonder if we would ever see one again.

"You're lucky to have Kit as a teacher," I said. "She was quite the gifted witch back in the old days."

If glares could kill, I'd be dead. "Girl, I could take you down in the blink of an eye, even without practice."

I grinned, though a shiver of apprehension rolled up my back. I didn't doubt she could do exactly that, but I never wanted to find out.

CHAPTER 9

Wednesday Afternoon

I had never been to another realm before. My parents taught Maddox and me about the Otherworld, the fae dimension that existed right alongside this human one, sharing details about the various creatures and fae inhabitants. My mom sometimes told us bedtime stories about the unseelie creatures that scared the shit out of me—particularly the ones that didn't look as human as the others, like the bogeyman or water-kelpies.

Knowing what I did now, I guessed that was her intent. Not that she was actively trying to give me nightmares or anything, but she wanted us to be prepared for the worst. Besides, I much preferred learning those things from her stories rather than a textbook. My brother would be able to rattle off all kinds of details from our studies because he had been the bookworm out of the two of us. But all I remembered was that it was a dangerous place for humans to be.

Good thing none of us going today was human.

Regardless of the dangers, I had a definite pep in my step as I followed Colin, Thane, and the blue-winged angel I now knew as Nathan around the side of Broderick Ó Faoláin's home, the duke who lost his life and nearly his soul to a crazed rogue reaper named Sophia. The queen opened one of the primary portals to and from the Otherworld in the duke's lush backyard, located in the upper-class Morningside neighborhood. The backyard was a veritable oasis complete with rock formations creating waterfalls that spilled into a pond. Lush vegetation surrounded the entire yard, keeping away any prying eyes.

After the duke's death, the property was turned over to the fae queen. She sent someone to maintain the grounds until she was convinced the duke's replacement wouldn't betray her as Broderick had by joining William. If only she had ensured her people's loyalty the first time around.

I hadn't seen Nathan since Xavier escaped from prison and tried to abduct me on the streets of Miami. Today, the angel pulled his long, dark brown hair back into a low ponytail and dressed similarly to Thane—black dress slacks, a button-down shirt, and shiny leather shoes. His wings, white with a bluish tint, were tucked close to his broad back. As a fighter, he was built like a tank and had at least an inch or two of height on Thane, not to mention some extra muscles.

"Please keep in mind that nothing will be as it seems," Colin warned as we approached a dense clump of ferns. "The realm is designed to keep non-fae out or trap them forever, whether they have a guide or not. My job is to simply get you through the gate as far as the magic is concerned. After that, it's up to each of you to stay focused."

I chewed on my lip as I eyed the ferns, knowing I was about to embark on the biggest adventure in recent times. As weird as the place was, the desert didn't count.

It took me a moment to realize all three men were staring at me as if waiting for something. "What?"

Thane took my hand and drew me to him, his heat washing through me and mixing with mine. He cupped the back of my neck with his other hand, and I was forced to look into his eyes. Those beautifully deep blue pits of desire. "Nathan and I will not be affected by the magic within the Otherworld." The spice of cardamom drifted off him to tease my senses. "So you're the only one who might be tempted to go wandering off."

"Except I'm a badass, remember?" Butterflies were dancing a jig in my stomach.

He smirked, his eyes drifting to my lips. "Prove it."

My mouth parted, breathless, too caught up in the warmth spreading through every pore of my body, simmering in my lower belly and between my legs, to think of a snarky reply. "Oh, I will."

When he let me go, I shivered against the rush of cooler air. Far from actually cold, but much cooler than my internal temperature at the moment. Colin's pale cheeks had a distinctive red flush to them, and his jaw moved as he clenched his teeth. I wanted to smirk. Served him right for keeping secrets from me.

The guilt was immediate, my stomach clenching in remorse at my callous thought. Working as a double agent, he had been keeping me as informed as he was allowed to. He was the good guy, a fact I needed to keep reminding myself. I gave him a small smile.

With a quick nod, he turned to the bushes and raised a hand, palm out. I sighed, hoping I hadn't pissed him off too much. The last thing I needed was another fae holding a grudge, especially when we were about to enter his world— one I knew next to nothing about.

The air in front of Colin's hand wavered and rippled outward like a drop of dew falling on still water. As the ripple grew, the air pulled apart, forming an oval-shaped portal we could step through as easily as a doorway. The other side was dark and misty, blocking any hint of what we'd actually be walking into.

Nathan went through first, a precaution in case anything not so nice waited on the other side. After squeezing my hand, Thane went through next, disappearing into the mists. My pulse raced as I raised my foot to follow, but Colin's hand on my arm held me back. I met his gaze, noting the sorrow in his blue-green eyes.

"I'm truly sorry for any deception, Veronica," he said truthfully. I knew it was true because the fae couldn't lie. "And I hope you'll consider forgiving me someday."

I sighed. "I already do, Colin, but I'm also stubborn as a fucking mule."

He let out a surprised laugh, and the corner of my lip twitched.

"We're good. I promise." I winked at him, then

followed the reaper and angel into fairyland.

Ice cold air brushed my skin as I moved through the portal. Dense fog and mist meant I couldn't see a damn thing in front of me, but I kept moving if only to get out of this freezing temperature. I rubbed my arms as I walked, tiny icicles forming on the skin beneath my palms. A quick glance behind me showed I was alone, or at least couldn't see more than a foot away, and both thoughts set my heart thumping against my ribs. I clenched my jaw as my teeth started to chatter.

Was it supposed to take this long? Did I get lost somehow? My breath hitched in my throat as I realized that was a genuine possibility. I had never gone through a portal before, and I hadn't thought to ask if I was supposed to do something or look for anything once inside. I'd have to hope Colin would have warned me.

Or maybe this was his way of punishing me.

The mists parted, and fierce relief washed the fear away. My shoulders relaxed as Thane and Nathan appeared.

At first glance, the Otherworld wasn't so different from the human world, just most definitely not Florida. Fields of green dotted the landscape around us, the path surrounded by towering trees that looked like pine or oak. Considering the branches' twists and turns, likely a non-human world variety. Far in the distance, a snow-capped mountain peeked above the tree line.

The similarities to the human realm ended there.

Every color splashed across this world seemed heightened and brightened, and every flutter of leaves caught my eye with their brilliance. It was like seeing the world through my falcon eyes, only while standing on two feet.

Disorienting and mesmerizing. The sun shone above in a cloudless, bluish-lilac sky, warming the air without the wetness of Miami. Birds chirped and cawed in the safety of the trees, but the calls were unlike any I'd heard before. The beauty of their song brought tears to my eyes, and I longed to join them.

A warm, familiar hand slipped into mine and squeezed. I returned the reaper's gesture but couldn't tear my gaze away from the landscape. "Have you been here before?"

"I've been to the Otherworld, but not the Summer Court," Thane said. "The Winter Court is as you would expect, and just as enhanced as it is here."

I shivered at the idea of entering a frozen world if the Winter Court had been ruling at this time. Huzzah for small victories.

"Follow me." Colin backed along the path curving between the trees. "And remember, do not touch or eat anything."

Since reapers and angels didn't eat or drink, that comment was just for me. I crinkled my nose. Like I would try to eat anything in the forest. Still entranced by my surroundings, I declined to comment before following the fae into the woods.

Despite Colin's warning, my fingers itched to reach out and touch everything in sight. A quick glance proved I was the only one suffering from this affliction. The angel and reaper easily kept pace with him, surveying our surroundings with serious expressions. This was their job, after all.

Technically it was my job, too, right now, but I hadn't died to get it. Well, I guess I did, but not in the way those two did.

We passed over an arched wooden bridge spanning a creek, and the bubbling of water gliding across rocks called to me, soothing my soul. I stepped closer to the side and glanced down. Usually only the ocean enticed me to visit, but here in this magical realm, this tiny strip of water cutting through the forest encouraged me to follow it to its source. I followed its winding path with my gaze instead. Maybe it ended in the ocean.

As we stepped off the bridge and the bubbling moved behind us, the Siren-like song of the water ceased. I shook my head, uneasy in its wake. If I was alone, I might have answered its call. Would I have been lost to these woods forever?

I shivered and moved a step closer to Thane.

A trio of yellow and white butterflies danced into the air as we passed their flowery perch. I smiled as they flitted around my head before heading off between the trees. As their dance moved through the foliage, my breath caught in my throat. From a small clearing between trees, a stag the color of midnight, the deep space between stars, stared back at me with eyes like starlight. His antlers were huge, the twinkling points brushing the leaves hanging from branches high above.

I raised a hand to stop the group, but I couldn't tear my gaze away from the majestic animal to see if they obeyed. I was entranced. The stag lowered his head slightly and chuffed, emitting a low puff of air.

Come, a sparkling voice rang in my head like tiny bells, *let us meet. I do not know your kind.*

My eyes widened in surprise, but my feet obeyed. Ferns and tall grasses brushed my legs and hands as I passed into the forest, heading for the stag. His gaze never left mine, and my heart thudded, not knowing whether this animal was friend or foe. My gut told me I was safe.

Put out your hand, he said when I was close enough to touch him. This close, his coat was pure velvet, not a single scar marring the canvas. Yes, this creature was a work of art.

I did as told, and he leaned his head down. The hairs along his soft nose tickled my palm as he sniffed it. When he looked up again, his exhale brushed the hair back from my face like a warm night's breeze. He smelled of juniper and moss.

I sense sun and fire in your blood, but your kind has not been seen here in many years. Why have you come?

"One of the fae, an unseelie of the Winter Court, attacks the human world," I explained as if speaking to a stag in the middle of the magical woods were completely normal. "We've come to ask for the queen's aid."

Why do you concern yourself with the realm of man?

"It's my home," I answered.

Mirognya is where you belong.

I furrowed my eyebrows. "Mir-what?"

"Veronica!" Thane's frantic call pulled my attention away from the stag. The reaper came crashing through the bushes a moment later, out of breath. His expression was one of fear and anger. "What the hell are you doing?"

"Talking to…" I gestured at the stag, who had disappeared. I blinked at the spot in the clearing where he had stood, the grass still bent where his hooves had been, and looked back up at Thane.

"Where or what is *Mirognya*?"

CHAPTER 10

Wednesday Afternoon

Thane stared at me for a moment, emotions I couldn't identify fast enough flashing through his eyes before he grabbed my hand and all but dragged me back toward the path. The tall grasses grabbed at my clothes as we passed.

"I'm holding your hand from now on," he said in an exasperated tone. "You don't leave my side. Understood?"

I glanced back at the clearing. Did any of that meeting actually occur, or did realm-hopping scramble my brain? "You didn't answer me."

"Because you're not making sense."

I frowned but kept my mouth shut. My meeting with

the stag had been anything but imaginary or coincidental, and a force deep within warned me to keep it to myself. I knew the stag wasn't harmful just as much as I knew I wasn't a cold-blooded murderer. I only killed when necessary, which had been a lot more often as of late. Regardless, I would ask someone more likely to have the answer when we returned—Adam. And he better fucking tell me, because I knew I did not just make that word up while traipsing around in fairyland.

Mirognya.

Colin and Nathan waited for us on the path beyond a group of trees huddled close together. The angel looked as serene and unperturbed as ever, but the fae let out a huge rush of air.

"Good grief, Veronica," Colin said. "I thought you would be able to resist the pull."

I narrowed my eyes. "Guess not. Let's get going now that I'm tethered to the dead guy." I held up our joined hands for emphasis. Joking about Thane's deceased nature was petty—and something I hadn't done in some time, I realized—but I was also trying to hide the tremble in my hand as my anger rose. Whatever had just happened with the stag hadn't been some sort of magical trick to get me lost forever. The animal knew what I was, and, like everyone else it seemed, knew more about my kind than I did.

First Jackson, the realm walker who killed my brother and was tasked with but failed at killing me, dropped the hint that there was more about who I was than I knew. Adam was sure as fuck keeping secrets, and now this stag in the middle of another fucking realm told me I belonged somewhere I had never heard of. The way the stag phrased his question about concerning myself with the realm of man made me believe *Mirognya* was another world. I wasn't a geography buff, but I knew for a fucking fact that it wasn't on any human map.

Why the hell had my parents kept so much a secret? What could possibly be so wrong about telling me more about where our kind came from and why we were the last? My cheeks and ears burned. Was *anything* I knew about myself real?

"We're here." Colin gestured ahead.

I tore my watering gaze away from the trees and gasped. We stood atop a hill, looking down into a valley. A city as big as central Miami and made of colorful crystal sat snug within the depths. From our vantage point, it was set up like a circle, with roadways spiraling toward the center. A lake drew up to the edge of the town on the left, its shimmering blue waves gently beating against the various docks and white-masted sailing ships. A mountain range sprawled out like a sleeping dragon behind the city.

In the middle of it all stood a building far taller than the rest. Spires twisted up toward the sun like unicorn horns, and smooth glass walls spread rainbows across the other buildings below.

The Summer Palace.

I probably could have spent all day there just staring at the city and taking it all in, but we had a job to do, which meant we wasted no time heading straight into the city of glass.

Time and distance moved differently in the Otherworld. What should have taken us a good hour on foot to get into the city only took a handful of minutes. No wall surrounded it as I would have expected, considering the fae's wild and fierce nature and need for dominance. But the Summerlands was far from helpless, as were the inhabitants.

A stone material that looked like cobblestone, but much glossier in texture, made up the roadways. Each stone was a shimmering gold, and I'd be lying if I said I didn't want to hum a song about the yellow brick road. The buildings were an odd mishmash of architectural styles, as if only parts of the city changed along with the human world. Despite the differences, everything was a brilliant white, reflecting the sun and making everything appear brighter.

The fae that lived here were mostly from the Summer and Spring Courts, although every once in a while, I caught the darker features of an Autumn Court member among the crowds. They all shared similar features which made it easy to determine who was who. The Spring Court—as in Colin's—was my favorite because their genetics included a variety of colors, such as bright blue eyes, light red hair that seemed almost pink in the right light, and freckles galore. One little girl even looked like an exact, though miniature, replica of my guardian angel Jessa.

I bit my lip, missing her even more. Hopefully we would get a chance to reconnect soon.

Because they had to make things even more complicated, the Summer Court also held members of the seelie, though not all Summer fae were seelie. Only a seelie fae could become queen or king. I wasn't completely sure what differentiated a seelie from a regular Summer Court member—likely special magical abilities or lack thereof— but I found it hilarious the human word "silly" came from seelie. Most fae were far from silly.

On the opposite spectrum were the fae of the Autumn and Winter courts, whose features reflected the more volatile seasons. The Winter Court fae were especially unusual in their colors, with cold, ice-like features—ranges of white or black hair, milky or dusky skin, and eyes that seemed to freeze you on the spot.

And while they were the cruelest in nature, due in part to being unseelie, much more dangerous among them were the boggarts, changelings, shades, and others whose names I'd forgotten. Because of their natural cruelty, no unseelie was permitted to step foot into the human realm, a precaution arranged to protect humankind. The angels would not have allowed any fae into the human world if the Summer Court king at the time of the realm-binding arrangement hadn't agreed.

Leave it to William to find a loophole.

For the most part, the fae folk paid us no mind, going about their business as we moved through the streets. In their own land, they allowed their wings to spread freely and used them to flit around. Unlike angel wings, theirs were a shimmering, gossamer texture reminiscent of butterflies. My fingers itched to touch them, to know if they felt as delicate as they looked, but that would be beyond rude—like touching someone's hair or pregnant belly without asking.

Maybe Colin would let me touch his. I crinkled my nose. That sounded so wrong. Even so, I peeked out of my periphery, but his wings were still hidden by a glamour.

I cocked my head. Why did he still hide them here?

To reach the towering palace's entrance, we crossed a behemoth of a bridge spanning parts of the city beneath. No guards stood at the gates, nor did any come out to stop our entry. Such precautions weren't necessary when the queen could seal the palace doors with a snap of her royal fingers. Using magic had always come to me without much effort—having a living flame residing in your core tended to do that—but the ease with which the fae used their abilities here in the Otherworld made me drool.

Our footsteps echoed against flawless marble floors and through empty hallways, and the only other fae who passed by paid us no attention. It was almost odd how little they noted our presence, but I guess that was the fae for you. When we reached the inner sanctum, closed doors that reached at least two stories high and the first armored guards we had seen blocked the way into what I assumed was the throne room.

"Colin Ó Broin here to see Queen Fiadh, along with three emissaries sent on behalf of the Archangel of Miami, Adam Larue," our fae guide said to one of the guards.

With a hand on the hilt of his sword, the guard's eyes roved over us, evaluating our potential threat level before giving a curt nod. He opened the door and stepped inside to announce us. Adam was right—the queen wouldn't turn down an angel's visit.

Entering the throne room, I had to clench my jaw closed so it wouldn't hang open in awe. Glass walls surrounded us, allowing a crystal-clear view out to the city and lake below and lighting up the space inside as if we were under the rays of the sun. A white marble floor with striking black veins spanned the length and width of the room and shone as if no particle of dust had ever dared to touch it. Nothing covered the pattern except a throne on a raised dais, upon which sat a fae woman of breathtaking beauty gazing down on us.

As much as I loved my own normally blonde locks, I had immediate hair envy. Hers was the color of the sun, a golden yellow so rich it sparkled like actual gold. It fell in thick waves down to the deep purple seat of the chair. Her eyes shone as brightly as a cloudless summer sky, her skin bronzed to perfection. No wrinkles appeared around her eyes or mouth, but I was sure this woman was at least as old as Xavier. As in a millennium or two, and still considered young to her own kind.

Power rippled off her in near-tangible waves, and an expertly crafted longbow and quiver of arrows stood within arm's distance. I had no doubt I'd find an arrow sticking out of my chest if I even hinted at making the wrong move. She also wore a suit of leather armor, complete with bracers and vambraces on her arms and legs. Golden threads wove through each piece, no doubt imbued with magic to further protect her. The symbols looked vaguely familiar, likely from my studies as a kid.

I grimaced as I made the connection. No, more like the symbols the necromancers carved into their victims. Yuck. Fae magic had officially been ruined for me.

Colin took a knee in front of the dais, but Thane and Nathan remained standing after a brief bow of respect. I followed their example with an awkward curtsy. We weren't her subjects, after all.

"Your Majesty," Colin began. "We come before you to discuss an urgent matter in the human realm. May I request a private audience?"

"Why should a matter amongst humans require privacy?" Her words dripped with disdain.

"Because it also concerns the fae. The archangel would prefer privacy as well."

The queen regarded each of us for a moment with a glossy gaze, almost like her thoughts weren't completely with us, before flicking her hand. The few fae milling around the room quickly departed, and the guard shut the door behind him. We were alone, though the queen was far from unprotected. "Continue."

"William Caomhánach has discovered the ways of shadow magic," Colin explained. "He intends to Raise an army of the dead to overtake the human enforcement agency, as well as your throne."

Man, he sure cut to the chase. But I had a feeling the queen would not sit long enough for a proper tale of the rise of modern necromancy, no matter how fascinating it might have been to me. Maddox would be so proud of my newfound interest in learning history.

"That hardly seems possible, even if what you say is true for the human world," the queen said. "There is no way for that unseelie to enter the Summerlands without my permission."

"The force he is creating and sending our way will crush any magical defenses we have here."

"Not possible." The queen's words were hollow and detached. The emptiness was unnerving. "No power is strong enough for that."

Thane stepped forward. "If I may, Your Majesty. The necromancer responsible is attempting to harness reaper magic."

Her Majesty was most definitely not expecting *that* response. Emotions fled from her face, leaving it as smooth and still as the glass walls surrounding us. "You have wasted your time coming here."

"But Your Majest—" Colin started, but with a flick of Queen Fiadh's wrist, guards appeared to escort us out.

"As I said before, such a task is not possible," she said. "I would welcome your stay, but I believe your *humans* have more need of you than I."

And with that, we were dismissed.

Back in the hall, I pursed my lips. Something felt off about that encounter. "Is she always like that?"

Colin frowned, his eyes deep in thought. "No, she was much more aloof and dismissive than usual."

"We didn't get a chance to tell her what happened at the stadium. We need to go back in."

I turned toward the door, but Thane's hand stopped me. "We knew this was a likely outcome. It's time to return to Miami."

I blinked at him. "So you just want to give up?"

"Politics aren't always easy, especially when it involves royalty."

"Then she was right. This was a complete waste of time." At least in this necromancer situation. I had learned something very valuable from the stag.

"Not necessarily," Thane said. "She is now aware of the threat and won't be able to claim otherwise later."

"Except no one was there to witness," I pointed out. "Besides us."

"The fae can't lie."

"No, but they're quite good at skirting around the truth." I worked really hard not to glance at Colin. "Besides, there might not be anyone alive later on to hold her accountable."

Doom and Gloom had become my new middle names.

Colin let out a sigh and ran a hand through his auburn hair. "I'll stay and continue to try and make her see reason. I've learned shadow magic myself, after all. A little show might do wonders."

Thane nodded and held out a hand. "Thank you. We appreciate your help. With any hope and a bit of luck, she'll come around."

Colin shook his hand grimly. "If not, I fear for both our worlds."

CHAPTER 11

Wednesday Evening

The new Master Vampire of Miami was actually a Vampiress—Lady Emilia Delacroix. I knew this because Adam sent Thane a text message while we were in the Otherworld, which the reaper saw when we returned and he turned his phone back on. Technology of any kind did not work in a logical fashion when traveling between realms. Days or months could pass before messages got through, and there was no way to tell if the words were even accurate. Best to shut devices off completely.

The archangel asked that we meet with Lady Emilia upon our return and convince her to aid our cause. Nathan left us to bring Adam up to speed on how the queen had reacted to our plea. I felt a bit like a gopher at this point, going wherever the archangel pointed. But we really were the right people for the task, having seen and experienced firsthand what the Society of the Dead was up to and how bad it was going to get if we didn't stop them soon. So I wouldn't complain too much.

Besides, this was fun. I just wouldn't tell Thane or Adam that.

"Why do we have to go in person? Can't we just call her?" Even though I *was* having fun, we had also been going nonstop since I returned from Tucson. My feet begged for a rest, and my stomach grumbled painfully. Facing another Master Vampire while tired and hungry had to be a bad idea.

"Diplomatic matters are best handled in person," Thane said as we approached the entryway to the luxury condominium the previous Master of Miami, Xavier, had purchased for the local hive.

The vampire who tried to add me to his collection of supernatural pretties may have fled the city, but all his assets were seized and turned back over to the king and queen of the North American Vampire Association. And now that they named a Mistress, she owned it all.

Shadows stretched long arms across the asphalt leading up to the building, and crickets began their evening serenade. The exterior of the eight-story condominium was painted tan and boasted balconies outside each residence. They even looked used, which was weird considering vampires hated daylight. Maybe they enjoyed the lights of the city at night like me, not that I wanted to compare myself to the bloodsuckers.

"Okay, but I'm going to need a huge fucking meal after

this." I walked through the door Thane held open, straight into the vampires' lair.

These beings were such an oddity in this world. Once human, they clawed their way out of their own graves after death—the unlucky ones did, in my opinion, the lucky ones stayed dead—only to find themselves looking and acting like a sickly, half-decayed creature from an old horror film. It took centuries for them to appear as they once did, only with supernaturally enhanced features to entice their prey closer until it was too late and dinner was served.

My stomach growled.

The new vampires would regain their human features *if* they survived long enough to become enhanced. Bloodlust was a powerful instinct and plenty of them succumbed to the feast against orders. If reaping souls didn't do it, cleaning up after vampires sure kept the DEA busy. I was lucky; in my relatively recent past life as an acquirer of the fantastical, I rarely had to deal with them. Until Xavier tricked me, that is.

Embroidered couches and chandeliers sparkling with hanging crystals that were most likely real diamonds filled the rectangular foyer. Hallways branched off to the right and left, but swinging doors like in an old-time saloon were installed to keep visiting eyes from seeing more than they should. A set of elevators off to the left of reception waited for the next victims—I mean, visitors.

The area was empty of vampires, likely due to the time of day, save for a single receptionist behind the desk. Her dark features were clearly human, indicating she was at least one hundred years old, give or take a few decades. She smiled brightly when we entered the building, which quickly turned into a menacing scowl as she caught our scent.

Nope, no humans here, honey.

"How may I help you today?" Regaining her composure, she smiled, this time with fangs. She might not have been one of the newly created anymore, but she was still young enough in vampire time to hang onto bad habits. She'd styled her black hair in a natural afro and wore a very low-cut white crop top that showed off her healthy endowments. Vampires were all about sex appeal.

Behind her head, a skull secured to the wall grinned down at me. It sat atop a spike, and a layer of grey and black ash covered the white bone. Above the skull was a plaque that read, "Never Forget." The artist wasn't creative enough to come up with his own catchphrase, I guess.

Either way, I was smart enough to keep my eye roll in check. For now.

"The Archangel of Miami has scheduled a meeting with your Mistress." Thane flashed a dashing smile. "Please let her know we've arrived."

The poor receptionist fell for his charm. She batted long, dark eyelashes his way before scampering off with a pep in her step and a wiggle to her hips. High-waisted jeans made her curves even more dangerous to unsuspecting prey or fang-bang wannabe groupies.

"Does no one use phones these days?" I groaned as my stomach started to eat itself.

Thane glanced at my stomach. "Why don't you go grab food while I speak with Emilia?"

I waved a hand dismissively. "Like I would let you handle this alone. You'd probably get abducted again."

He rolled his eyes. "I can handle myself just fine. We're

here on official business.”

“And yet I still had to save your ass back at the stadium.” I crossed my arms, hoping the gesture would also silence my belly, or at least muffle the grumbling sounds. “I’m staying.”

“The Mistress will see you now,” the receptionist’s voice came from behind us, making me jump slightly. A good reminder that we were never truly alone here, and also that vampires were inhumanly fast and fucking sneaky.

We followed her to the nearest elevator and stepped inside. For the most part, she remained ambivalent, though I could have sworn she pushed her boobs up in her bra from the last time we saw her. About halfway to the eighth floor, her nostrils flared, and she turned to look at me. Her eyes narrowed.

“You’re not a reaper.” It wasn’t a question.

I raised an eyebrow. “It took you this long to figure out?”

Thane elbowed me in the side as her face crumbled. Who knew a vampire could be so sensitive.

“Sorry,” I said. “I’m just a really hungry shifter.”

The door of the elevator slid open before it got awkward again and the vampire held out a hand for us to exit. She remained inside. As the door slid shut again, I caught the wink she threw to Thane. No judgment from me, of course—the man was insanely hot.

I turned my attention to our surroundings. The top level had been converted into one giant penthouse that definitely put mine to shame. Not that I was competing with the vampires or anything, but that was how enormous and lavish this place was. Emilia wasted no time redecorating with red velvets, black and white furniture including a checkerboard tile floor, and random pieces of art and statues.

Actually, come to think of it, this might have been how Xavier decorated for all I knew. Whoever the designer was, it wasn't my style.

Kneeling atop the red velvet comforter of a custom-sized bed that had to have been larger than a California King was a woman facing us. A *naked* woman with lily-white skin and deep brown hair that caressed her skin almost down to her hips. She wasn't alone, I realized, and she wasn't just kneeling. She was straddling a man who was busy bucking his hips against hers.

What the fuck? They were…fucking. I was *not* prepared for this kind of meeting. I licked my lips, my mouth running dry as I watched. There was nothing else I could do; I was glued to the show.

The woman opened her eyes, striking light brown irises boring deep into mine. "Please, come in," she said, her voice husky and breathless. She continued to move with the man, who didn't even notice our appearance in the middle of his act. Letting out a small moan, she trailed her hands up her body to her nipples. "We'll be done soon. Unless you wish to join us?"

My body throbbed with a sudden need, and I took a step forward. A hand on my arm stopped me. Thane's expression was tense, beads of sweat breaking out on his forehead.

"We aren't here for pleasure," he said to the vampiress. "Just business."

The urge to join them dissipated. I realized my blouse had been halfway over my head, and I hastily pushed it back into place. Despite the disappearance of the unnatural desire, my lady bits still throbbed. Just fucking great. This was what I got for showing up at a vampires' nest while exhausted and starving.

"Pity," she cooed before climbing off the man. "We'll finish later, darling." She patted him on his muscular butt in a playful dismissal as he stood from the bed.

I couldn't help myself—I totally eyed his shapely behind as he sauntered away. I mean, who wouldn't? It wasn't like he was trying to hide it or anything.

Emilia pulled on a black silk robe before sliding off the side of the bed, though she didn't bother tying the front. I didn't know why she bothered with a robe in the first place after the little show she put on for us, and the fabric barely covered her ass. She was tall and lithe, moving with a dancer's grace to a seating area. Splotches of flushed skin peeked out from beneath the fabric, a sure sign she ate before her sexcapade. Or maybe even during.

She took a seat on a red velvet chaise and waved us over to join her. Stretching out comfortably to lounge, she addressed Thane, "I can only assume you're here about the Risen."

The reaper cleared his throat. "Yes. The Archangel is requesting all Community leaders' assistance in putting a swift end to the Society."

"Is it true about the fae's involvement?" She tilted her head to one side.

"It's true the current leader of the Society is an unseelie fae and that he has convinced several others to join him," Thane said carefully.

"Let me guess, he wants to use the Risen to go after his

queen." She laughed when Thane nodded. "So predictable."

"It would be in the vampires' best interest to help us rid the world of this threat. Not only do the Risen threaten your food source, but imagine if we could no longer control our presence in the shadows and humans became aware."

Her eyes narrowed. "We do not fear humans."

"Maybe you should," I said. "There's a hell of a lot more of them than us, and many of them like to use big fucking guns. Second amendment rights and all that."

Emilia's piercing gaze fell on me, and she smiled. Her lips were soft and plump and the same deep hue as a delicious red apple. Just as bitable, too.

I closed my eyes for a brief moment and took a deep breath, knowing then that she was toying with me again, using my pheromones against me.

"Humans may be plentiful, but they are weak, terrified of such tiny things as spiders and snakes." Her lip pulled up into a look of disgust. "They shriek at the mere sight of a mouse."

"The DEA spends a significant amount of time cleaning up after the vampires," Thane said. "Isn't it about time you all repaid the favor?"

"We will assist in tracking down the Risen as they come out of hiding and threaten the Community's existence." She smiled, though it was a far cry from friendly. "That is a requirement of the agency that we're willing to obey. But because the fae are involved, we will not fight. We will not go to war against the Otherworld."

"It's not all of the fae or even ones sanctioned by the queen," I argued, glaring at her. "In fact, the queen doesn't even think what they're doing is possible."

"Nevertheless, little bird, we will abstain from war." Her eyes flashed with desire as she used Xavier's pet name for me.

My skin crawled with rising goosebumps. How did she know about that name?

"Did you enjoy my new art piece at reception?" she asked. "I thought it a good reminder of what happens to traitors to our kind."

I blinked, my heartbeat pulsing faster. "Was that…?"

"Oh yes, Xavier's head makes a beautiful display, don't you agree?" She smiled like a cat eyeing its prey. "My gift to you."

So the ex-Master Vampire had met his tragic end at last, and I didn't know how I felt about that. I clenched my fists in triumph as much as frustration that it hadn't been by my hand. After everything Xavier put me through, I wanted to witness his death at least, to be sure of it. I wanted to see him turn to nothing but ash and bone.

Emilia's behavior tonight was unsettling, and I wasn't convinced she was telling the truth about Xavier.

But would she have a reason to lie?

CHAPTER 12

Wednesday Night

O kay, now I really need a giant fucking burrito or something," I said after we were back in the parking lot of the vampires' sanctuary. "With extra cheese and meat."

My stomach stopped grumbling a while ago thanks to that bizarrely arousing encounter we had walked in on, but now I needed a distraction from lingering desire still clenching at my body. Not to mention the bomb Emilia dropped that Xavier was officially dead, *if* she was telling the truth.

You would think that bit of news would be enough to quench the heat in my body, but no. Now I wanted to celebrate—with sex. I had problems.

Streetlights had flickered to life while we were inside, and the sun finished its descent beyond the horizon. No stars twinkled since we were in the middle of a city full of lights, but the moon shone brightly as we climbed back into my rental car. The plain sedan was a poor replacement for my baby, but it would get us back to my penthouse. There was a really good fast-casual place nearby where we could grab something to eat. Or at least I could.

Thane was deep in thought, rubbing his chin as he gazed out the window. I tried to relax, but all I could think about was sex. How much I wasn't getting, how much I wanted to get some, how much I wanted Thane, and even how much I considered going back and taking the Mistress up on her offer. Whatever enhancement Emilia had done to lure me closer left a horrible itch that needed scratching. A good, deep, satisfying scratch. I licked my lips.

A spark of fire touched my hand, flaring to life across my body—Thane's hand on mine.

"You in there?" he asked.

I took a shuddering breath. "Yeah, sorry, lost in thoughts." And if I didn't pull my hand away soon, I was going to make one giant fucking mistake. No pun intended. Or maybe it was. My head was a foggy mess of desire. Luckily, I needed to turn the wheel, and I pulled my hand out from under his. "What the fuck was that in there?"

"Vampires aren't exactly known for their selfless or generous nature."

"No, I mean with the sex." My body tingled with the word. "She knew we were coming." Just not literally.

He let out a laugh, a deliciously deep, robust sound.

"Typical. The older they get, the more bored they become. I wouldn't be shocked to receive an invitation to join her harem. Turning a reaper would make her a legend among her kind."

My nostrils flared at the idea of Thane becoming one of her pets, one of her fuck boys. He was *mine*.

I blinked. Where the hell had that possessiveness come from?

"Adam has teams reaching out to some of the smaller Community groups like the various shifters and lesser fairy kinds such as pixies," he said as I steered the car into the penthouse's parking garage. "We're off the hook for now."

Uh oh. Free time, a once desirable state of being now caused me mild anxiety thanks to the damn vampire encounter.

"Adam was able to remove the majority of the bounties out on you, but we're sure there are others we can't access," he continued. "And some will just ignore his command."

I parked in my assigned spot on the main level, and we climbed out of the car, strolling back toward the busy street and nearby restaurant. His hand slipped into mine, electric tingles shooting up my arm and down toward my belly. My brain was full of fuzz being this close to Thane. Hunger, exhaustion, and desire were clouding my every thought.

I was drunk, just not from booze.

At some point, I leaned my head on his shoulder, closing my heavy eyelids and allowing him to lead the way. For a few fleeting moments, it felt like we were a regular human couple out for an evening stroll. Until I stumbled on a crack in the sidewalk's cement, and my free hand reached out to grab something to catch myself. His bicep. His well-muscled bicep beneath his button-down shirt, tanned skin tight across the muscles of his forearms.

My breath came out in shallow gulps as I moved my hand down his arm, following the lines of his veins until I touched his belt. He wore far too nice of clothes for the thoughts racing through my mind, and I wanted to rip them off him. I raised my gaze to meet his ravenous one.

The next thing I knew we were in an alley. He pinned me against the wall, the rough brick scratching my back through my blouse. Both his hands slipped beneath my ass and lifted me, and I wrapped my legs around his waist for support. His obvious state of arousal pressed against the sensitive skin between my thighs, making me gasp and curse the clothing blocking us from truly touching.

"You're not the only one who wants this to happen," Thane growled in my ear, nipping at my lobe before moving down my neck.

I let out a soft moan. "I'm not fucking you in an alley." My voice was hoarse, and I wasn't actually sure if I believed myself. The darkness would keep us hidden from any peeping Toms.

"Are you sure about that?" He brought his head up, meeting my gaze as he smirked. Barely restrained hunger swam in his dark blue eyes. Gripping my hips tighter, he pulled me even more against him, moving me up and down his length straining against his pants.

Even through the layers of clothes, my body went wild, turning molten as desire and need built deep within, begging for release. I dug my fingernails into his shoulders before wrapping my arms around the back of his neck, pulling him closer. I kissed him hard, soft moans escaping my mouth as he continued to move my hips. I swear, a few more strokes, and I would come right then and there.

One hand moved away from his tight grip on my hips, and a moment later he pulled his head back to show me his teleportation device. "Just say the word and we can be back at your place."

My breath still came out in gasps as I met his gaze, his eyes a lighter sapphire than I'd ever seen before. He wanted me as much as I wanted him, and we both knew it was a deeper desire than just sex. Something bound us together.

But ours was a bond that could never last. We were Romeo and Juliet, except it was our species that kept us apart rather than our families. We could be together physically, fast and furious as much as we wanted and needed, but that was all we could ever be. I both needed and wanted to have children someday, and a reaper wasn't capable of such a task. The phoenix ritual intended for procreation didn't allow for modern advances in science; it had to be a physical act of mating.

I definitely needed to have a conversation with my gods to fix that. If only they listened to my prayers.

Thane lowered his head to my shoulder, kissing along my collarbone. His breath sent the tiny hairs on my skin fluttering, and shock waves rippled through my body to gather between my legs once again. I needed to have him. Death and destiny be damned.

An agonized scream rent the air, and I nearly tumbled to the ground in my effort to get back on my feet. Thane and I ran in the direction of the scream, the steamy moment forgotten for now.

It didn't take a genius or even an expert tracker to find

the source. Back on the main street, people ran away from an open area near a storefront, their cries and yells adding to the cacophony of noise along the road. As we approached, still at a run, the humans around us began to slow their pace, their faces clearing of fear. Thane activated his reaper repellant, which meant no human cops to worry about just yet. As in Tucson, a group of at least seven people—most likely mages though they were in normal clothing rather than their distinctive robes—surrounded a figure kneeling on the ground.

Only this wasn't another reaper.

Oh no…

It was an angel, her arms raised to ward off a blow from a jeweled dagger. One of the Daggers of Abaddon.

Fuck.

I nearly lost my footing when I realized what the mages were trying to do. Attacking and kidnapping an angel deserved a place in the lowest level of their hell, and I was happy to send them to an early grave. I could only assume they were going to try to harness her magic or kill her by trying.

My blades were free of their sheaths before I took my next breath, and I slammed into the closest mage. The fury of a phoenix released itself on these idiots who followed an unseelie fae daring to defile our realms with the undead.

I whirled around to the man's front while he stumbled and slashed. My blade carved a path through the mage's throat. Blood gushed out in a torrent, and I pushed him to the side.

A spell slammed into me, throwing me against the front of a store. Pain rattled through my skull as my head hit the metal frame beside the glass windows, followed by a sharp pain in my butt as I fell to the ground. I threw myself forward into a roll as another spell crashed into the storefront window, shattering the glass which rained down around me. I shook off the glass and leaped to my feet, throwing one of my knives at the spell-caster in the same move. She deflected it with a wave of her hand.

Shit. She was more powerful than I gave her credit for.

A flash of light caught my attention for a brief moment—the Reaper's Scythe reflecting a streetlamp's glow before cleaving its way through a mage from shoulder to opposite hip. The man's body slid to the ground in two halves.

The woman I fought paled as she watched her peer fall into literal pieces. It was enough of a distraction for me to catch her off guard. I closed in fast and sliced at her arm with my blade. The poison acted swiftly, incapacitating her within seconds. I ducked beneath a spell from another mage, then swept my leg out to knock him off his feet. I gave him a few quick nicks, deep enough to draw blood, ensuring he stayed down.

Within a handful of minutes, we had the mages defeated. Three were dead, three more knocked out or paralyzed with my poison, and one escaped—the one with the dagger that was capable of killing reapers and taking down angels.

Fuck.

I fell to my knees beside the crumpled angel. Long blonde hair covered her still face. My arms hung limp at my sides though I still clenched my knives in my fists. My chest heaved as I panted, letting my head fall forward as the truth revealed itself.

A pool of blood seeped out from beneath the angel.

We were too late.

CHAPTER 13

Wednesday Night

The air around us grew thin, making it even harder to take a breath. A moment later, a squadron of reapers stepped out of their teleporting circles. I didn't even notice Thane making a call. Warm hands took hold of my arms and led me away from the angel's body, giving the team room to get her and the others back to the agency.

I was beyond exhausted, my body trembling from the exertion of going too hard for too long. Hunger fled long ago, and now all I wanted was to curl up and sleep the pain and grief away. My heart felt heavy within my chest.

Why the fuck did they go after an angel? Regardless of Community political affiliations or religious beliefs, no one could deny the absolute beauty and holiness of the majestic creatures governing the human realm. Did they really think they could use her magic to create more Risen? How much farther were they willing to go?

I leaned against Thane's chest and closed my eyes as the world fell away, opening them a second later to find myself in my penthouse bedroom. Thane tucked his t-port device into his pocket and led me by the hand to the bathroom. He turned the shower on as hot as it could go and stepped toward the door. "Shower, then bed. No arguing."

I wasn't planning to. The bathroom door clicked shut behind me. I stripped off my clothes and stepped into the shower, relishing the burn of the water that washed the blood and grime away. I was too tired to cry, but my heart and lungs ached, hurting for those who already lost their lives to the Society of the Dead, as well as for the actions I was forced to take to protect others. It was a cruel conundrum to have, taking lives to save others. But it was when we stopped caring about the lives lost that we turned into the real monsters. Monsters like William.

Letting out a deep sigh as I finished scrubbing away the day, I stepped out of the shower and toweled dry. When I was dressed in my pajamas—as usual, a silk camisole and matching bottoms—and ready to fall into a deep slumber, I returned to my room. Thane stood at the sliding glass door leading onto the terrace, his hands tucked into his pockets and gazing out beneath furrowed brows. Moonlight shone across his profile, accentuating his already beautiful features with deep shadows.

"Stay with me?" I barely spoke the words, but he turned to face me. My breath caught in my throat. Gods, he was gorgeous. Not just that, though. Not anymore. He was a good man. Not perfect, but *good*. Decent. It didn't matter anymore that he had died once. Someday soon, he would earn his wings and be out of my reach forever.

It was time to make the most of today.

I crossed the room in the blink of an eye, running my hands up the hard planes of his chest to his neck and his hair. As I tangled my fingers in those luscious dark locks that had first caught my eye, I pulled his mouth to mine and crushed our lips together. He responded without hesitation; his hands encircled my bare waist as my top rode up, pulling our bodies closer and sending goosebumps across my skin. His touch was scorching, a heat calling to and teasing my inner fire.

I nipped at his lips before allowing his tongue to explore my opened mouth. He stole my breath as surely as he had stolen my heart. The kiss turned hungrier, and I gripped his hair tighter as he pushed my pajama bottoms to the floor. We broke apart for a moment so he could pull my camisole above my head, tossing it aside and leaving me in nothing but my panties.

His eyes roved over my nearly naked body, drinking almost every inch of me in. His clothes came next, my fingers practically ripping his belt buckle apart in my haste. When his pants hit the floor, he lifted me, wrapping my legs around his waist. The length of his stiff member rubbed against my body's most sensitive part through the fabric of my underwear. A moan climbed up my throat.

He carried us both to the bed, our lips locked together once again. Somehow I found my back on the sheets and a pillow beneath my head, but those things wouldn't have mattered to me in my current state of need. Yes, I needed this man. I didn't know why or what force was driving our connection so intensely, but I didn't care anymore. Nothing mattered but him.

His lips found their way to my ear, and he whispered, "Tonight, we take care of you."

Then he kissed his way down my body, trailing nips and licks across the rise and fall of my chest, circling my nipples, which rose hard and taut beneath his touch. My breaths came out fast, and I tangled my fingers in his hair as he moved farther south, needing to grasp at something as the ache increased inside the lowest part of my belly.

When he reached my legs, he leaned back and slowly pulled my underwear down over my thighs and calves, his gaze never leaving mine. The wicked gleam in his eyes spoke to the levels of pleasure I was about to receive, and I shuddered in excited anticipation. There would be no argument from me about making things equal. Not tonight. His gaze moved down my body to the softest, most intimate area. A smirk pulled up his lips.

That goddamn smirk. But before I had a chance to say something snarky, his mouth was on me, his tongue flicking and sucking. Everything else around me faded as the living flame inside of me went wild. Every inch of me was molten and sparking like a live wire as a hot knot of pleasure grew between my legs. I fisted his hair, holding him in place as if it would somehow ground me. The pressure built, overwhelming and incredible with each stroke, each suck, until the dam burst. My body bucked in response, and I cried out.

Sun and flames, I needed that.

I rolled over onto my back, my arm landing on an empty bed beside me. Beneath furrowed brows, I opened my eyes, squinting against the bright light of the room.

No reaper. Did he run out on me?

My mouth felt like sandpaper. I sat up, swinging my legs down to the floor. A full glass of water waited on my nightstand. At least he had been thoughtful before leaving. I drank it down in one long gulp before getting to my feet and heading for the bathroom, still naked. I sure made a mess of things. It had been a delightfully delicious mess until I passed out after I orgasmed, but now what?

Memories of our passion came back to me hard and fast, much like I wanted him inside me, and desire stoked low in my belly. I squeezed my legs together, fervently wishing that man's mouth and hands were still all over me.

Who was the junkie now?

After splashing cold water on my face and tossing my hair up into a messy bun, I turned toward my closet, stopping as I caught a glance of myself in the mirror. A splotchy, red mark marred the skin above my left boob, under my collarbone. I frowned and rubbed at it, not able to recall any specific injury from the fight or the pleasure between the sheets. It didn't hurt to touch, either.

Oh well. Hazards of the job.

I marched my naked ass into the closet and pulled on some linen shorts and a tank top. Thanks to Jessa's foresight, my kitchen was full of newly purchased food and beckoned to me as hunger threatened to claw itself loose. I hadn't had that damn burrito I wanted the night before.

I stopped mid-step in my living room, my mouth popping open as I caught sight of Thane lounging casually on my L-shaped couch. He was back in his daily attire of slacks and a button-down, though these appeared to be a different pair than the night before, and a newspaper covered most of his face as he read. "I thought you left."

He looked up from the paper and smirked. "Why, Veronica, I had no idea you thought so poorly of me."

I held up a hand to stop him from any further talking and sniffed the air. "Did you get burritos?"

"In the kitchen." He raised the paper again. "You seemed pretty bummed about not getting one last night, so I ordered delivery."

My feet were rooted in place, my mouth hanging agape. I was coming to the quick conclusion that this man was not who I once thought he was. Or maybe he had changed. Or perhaps I was just that desirable.

Yeah, that must be it. So desirable that this man ordered me a burrito for breakfast, hoping to make things equal now that I was rested and would soon be a lot less hungry. As a firm believer in equality for all, I was definitely okay with that.

I snapped my mouth shut and entered the kitchen, digging into the plastic to-go bag without delay. I took a giant bite out of the monstrous, goodness-filled tortilla and moaned in pleasure. It was entirely possible that this burrito was better than the orgasm the night before. Too close to tell for sure.

Burrito in one hand and a plate in the other, I padded back to the living room and sat near Thane, close enough to bump knees.

"When you're finished eating, we're headed to the morgue to see Owen," he said without looking up. "He has some theories about the angel's death."

And just like that, my breakfast was ruined. Not because of the angel's death—no, I still felt a keen sense of loss and grief from arriving too late to help. But this burrito ruining moment was because the morgue brought up images of the last time we visited, and the three decaying Risen bodies we had to study. Were reapers completely unaware of how unappetizing dead things were?

Well, genuinely dead, anyway. Thane's lips and tongue had been quite appetizing the night before, and I was very content with the outcome of no longer viewing his death as a hindrance to our intimacy. Tingles rushed down my body. This was most definitely not the right time to be thinking about *that* anymore. But… did we need to get the elephant out of the room?

"Thanks for last night." I set the plate and burrito on the coffee table, giving the tortilla one last longing glance.

The reaper folded up his paper and regarded me. I couldn't read his expression, but if I had to guess, I'd say it was a mix of amusement and pride. "You're welcome. But don't think you're off the hook. I expect the favor returned."

I raised an eyebrow, my pulse quickening beneath his gaze. "Oh, you do, huh? Why didn't you just join in?"

The look in his eyes turned smoldering, my lady bits instantly throbbing in response. "When I have you for the first time, I want you at full capacity." He leaned closer, his hands sliding up my bare legs along with warm tingles that sent a shiver of pleasure up my spine. "I intend to spend hours tiring you out myself."

My brain was too fuzzy to form a reply, so I just stared at him. The first time. He said the first time, which meant he knew as well as I did that this thing between us wouldn't just be a one-night stand.

His hands continued to rise up my thighs and beneath my shorts until his thumbs dipped beneath the band of my panties. I closed my eyes with a soft moan, or possibly a whimper, ready to lie back and let him have his delicious way with me.

But instead, he withdrew, his sudden disappearance a shock to my system. My eyes flew open to find him smirking at me once again.

"That day isn't today." He rose to his feet. "We have an appointment."

That smug motherfucker.

CHAPTER 14

Thursday Morning

When we arrived inside the lower level of the DEA building downtown, Dr. Owen Cooper was waiting for us, a stack of folders and a tablet in hand. As before, his blond hair and sparkling blue eyes spoke to the youth he was before he died and found himself working for Adam. Poor kid. I wondered what had happened to him, but it wasn't polite to ask, even if I was pretty sure Owen would love to tell me all about any gory or gruesome details. He made for the perfect mortician.

"Ah, Veronica, such a pleasure to see you again." His eyes lit up when he saw me, and he held out a hand. "I promise I washed them."

I smiled at his joke and shook his offered hand. "Someday we'll have to meet under less depressing circumstances." I had an inkling he would be a heck of a lot of fun at a club or pulling pranks on his coworkers.

His expression sobered. "Yes, the death tolls have been far too high to handle appropriately. And now an angel? Adam has promised help, but when we're dropping like flies…" He let the thought trickle out. "Anyway, let's chat." He waved at us to follow him into the back of the morgue.

Before we left my place, I changed into joggers and pulled on a zip-up hoodie, and I was so glad I did. Sure, I ran hotter internally than the average human, but cooler temps had a biting reaction against my phoenix skin. Hence why Miami would always be home.

Thankfully, Owen didn't lead us into the morgue's actual lab but stopped inside the viewing room. Today a thick black curtain covered the window on the right where they displayed bodies for identification or even a final farewell. I turned away from it, not wanting to know what was behind the curtain and hoping to keep my memories of Maddox at bay.

The doctor motioned us to sit on the blue couch on the other side of the room, and he took a chair across the coffee table. "I'm sure this goes without saying, but what we discuss here needs to stay between the three of us. Adam is adamant that this situation remain as quiet as possible, and for good reason."

While it would be easy to rile the Community up with news of the angel's death, it was also bad for business to share that it was possible. Most of us thought angels were invincible—myself included, until these Daggers came along.

"Of course." I had every intention of obeying, and I was also eager as fuck to find out whatever secret the doc was about to reveal.

"Kara wasn't the first angel to be attacked." Owen removed photos from one of the folders, set two on the coffee table, and turned them so we could see the pictures right side up.

I gasped and quickly closed my eyes, but the images seared into my memories, where they would remain for the rest of my days. Like the bodies of the Risen we saw in the morgue previously, this angel's skin had been hacked into, symbols carved into his skin. But the necromancers had gone a step further with this angel—they had removed his wings, just like Broderick.

I shuddered. What the fuck was wrong with these people?

"It's gruesome, I know, but we assume they removed his wings with a Dagger of Abaddon to keep him from escaping."

I nodded and took a deep breath before opening my eyes and studying the photos, doing my best to keep my gaze glued to the symbols carved into the angel's flesh and nothing else. "Are they seriously trying to Raise an angel?"

"I don't believe so." Owen pulled out a few more photos, this time of human Risen. He pointed to the differences in the symbols. "It's true that each mage carves their Risen with unique markings to bond themselves to the body. But there's a significant difference here."

"Any ideas?" Thane asked.

"My best guess is that they're trying to harness the angel's magic somehow. Perhaps they believe it will enable faster Raisings or more than one at a time?"

Goosebumps raced up my arms and neck. Did these mages have no shame? No morals?

Apparently not.

"Do you have any reason to believe that theory to be accurate?" Thane asked.

Owen tapped a finger against his chin. "No matter how unlikely, I can't completely rule it out yet."

My stomach clenched. Ugh. This just kept getting worse and worse. I needed to keep the conversation moving so I didn't focus on my roiling guts. "Did you find out anything from the reaper's extracted memories? The one from Tucson?"

"Nothing that would help, I'm afraid," Owen said. "Just confirmation that he'd been held against his will. Their goal was to harness his magic as we thought."

"So, they tracked him down in Tucson?"

The doctor nodded. "They tortured your location out of him, so he was coming to take you back to Miami. You saved him from a far worse fate, if it's any consolation."

It wasn't, but I appreciated him for trying. That reaper had saved my life. I wished I could have done the same for him. So much death and destruction. "Have we heard from Colin yet? Any success with convincing the queen?"

Thane shook his head. "He's due to check in with Adam later today."

"What I still don't understand is how William convinced a realm walker to work for him," I said. "What the hell could he have promised that would be enticing enough?" Another good question Jackson Reed never answered—what the fuck had that realm walker gotten in exchange for killing Maddox, and from whom?

I ground my teeth together.

"Could be as simple as money, titles, or power," Thane said. "If William was able to tap into dark enough magic to access necromancy, then it's likely he discovered something that tempted a power-hungry realm walker."

"Are all the unseelie able to enter now?" I asked.

"Only in ones and twos as the realm walker brings them over," Owen said. "We would have even more of a problem on our hands if the entire barrier came down. The various types of unseelie rival the demons for their level of evil."

My body gave a quick shudder as a shiver ran up my spine. Unleashing more evil in this world was not something I wanted to see, and there had been way too many unseelie for anyone's comfort at the stadium. All members of the Winter Court were unseelie, but there were other kinds than just the human-looking ones, and far more disturbing in nature. Changelings, for example, took the place of human children, unbeknownst to the parents until their once well-behaved child turned into an uncontrollable hellion or a sadistic sociopath. I was willing to bet that most serial killers weren't actually human.

And the children who were whisked away to the Otherworld? Well, let's just say there's a reason you shouldn't eat anything when visiting the Winterlands.

"Do you think it's possible to bring down the whole barrier?" I asked.

Thane met my gaze. "Yes."

"Maybe that's what William is trying to do by

harnessing the angels' magic. Maybe he's moved on from just using the Risen to bring down the DEA. Releasing the unseelie would be catastrophic to this world."

Owen released a low whistle. "That's for sure."

Thane's cell phone buzzed. As he checked the message, his face darkened, and he quickly rose to his feet. "We need to go. Another angel has been taken."

CHAPTER 15

Thursday Morning

"How is this even possible?" I asked as Thane withdrew his t-port device from his pocket. "Aren't angels more powerful than mages?"

"A few against one, yes, but even angels have their limits, especially if the mages use a Dagger." He took my hand, pulling me to my feet, and glanced at Owen. "Keep looking. We need to know what William intends to do if we're right about the unseelie."

The mortician nodded, his expression grim.

We stepped inside the holographic teleportation circle, and my insides pulled apart. A moment later, we were on the streets of Miami outside a two-story high school. My molecules bound themselves back together in a rush. It was getting more manageable, but I still had to gulp down stomach acid trying to rise, grimacing against the burn.

"Adam sent me the coordinates of the angel's last known location." Thane frowned as he looked around. "It was only a few minutes ago, so they couldn't have taken the angel far."

An agonized scream ripped from within the school building, which should have been empty for summer. The anguished sound sent shivers down my spine, and I hoped we weren't too late like before. We ran for the closest door, and Thane practically ripped it off its hinges as he pulled.

The vast halls were empty save for rows of blue lockers, but I had knives in hand, ready to attack. Another wail came from up the stairs, making my insides clench painfully. Our footsteps echoed down the corridor as we raced for the stairwell, taking the steps quickly but hugging the wall as we neared the second level. A door halfway down the next hall was open, fluorescent light streaming out onto the linoleum floor.

I bit my lip as the screams rose in pitch, urging myself not to run straight in without assessing the danger first. I crept low, my knives ready to be thrown. Reaching the door, I held a hand up to Thane to wait. He nodded, and I took a deep breath, inching forward until the room was visible.

At least six mages in their stupid black and red ceremonial robes and the angel on the ground, face down. Two held her pearlescent pink wings tight in their hands. Another knelt over her with one of those damned Daggers of Abaddon. No wonder they had been able to take down angels. I clenched the knife in my fist. We needed to get the last two Daggers away from them.

A mage shifted, and I caught a glimpse of the angel's fiery red hair. My blood ran cold, and I threw my arm over my mouth to keep from crying out, pulling back quickly to avoid being seen. Thane's hand gripped my shoulder to keep me from falling.

That angel was Jessa—my guardian angel with the lagoon-colored eyes.

Oh, *hell* no.

My fists tightened on the handles of my blades as fury rippled through my body. No more waiting. I nodded to Thane and bolted inside.

I threw my knives, both of which found targets in human or fae flesh, and drew two more. If the first two hits didn't kill them, the poison would still incapacitate them. This time, I unleashed my inner flame, looping a wire-like strand around the hilt of a knife and releasing it toward a mage. I pushed the flame outward, forming a fiery whip that ended in a razor-sharp blade. I cracked my hand down and the whip followed, slashing at the closest mage and slicing through an eye.

The stench of sizzling skin filled the air, and he stumbled backward with his hands over his face, screaming. I whirled and slashed again and again, letting the fire and steel maim whoever moved into their path. In my other fist, I used the second knife to slice and paralyze with the poison coating its blade.

Thane followed me in at some point, but all my attention was on the mages. How dare they attack any angel, let alone this angel? *My* angel.

They would pay for this. William was a dead man.

When the last of the mages fell, she writhed in pain until the poison took hold, and she went stock still. My fiery whip dropped and dissipated into ash, and the blade clattered to the floor. I rushed to Jessa's side, sheathing my other knife. One of her wings drooped, halfway cut away from her back. As gently as possible, I turned Jessa in my arms, ignoring the blood smearing across my lap.

Her blue-green eyes fluttered open, and she struggled to focus on my face.

"Oh, Jessa." My voice broke, coming out as little more than a whisper. "I'm so sorry."

Thane's teleportation device clicked as his scythe retracted, and he tucked the cylinder away into his pocket. He knelt beside us and took Jessa's hand in his.

The angel's gaze remained on my face until recognition flickered to life behind her eyes. "Veronica," she said, then grimaced. "You need to leave. Now. This is…" She gasped for air as a spasm rocked through her body. "Set up…for you."

Back on his feet in a flash, Thane withdrew his device and activated the teleportation circle. A blast of ice rocked through the doorway and threw me sideways. I struggled to get back up, my limbs succumbing to the cold. Each move was sluggish. I heated myself from within until steam rose from my skin. Conjuring my inner flame again, I threw a fireball at the door. Whoever was out there was not a friend.

Wood and drywall blew outward from the explosion, and the remainder of the doorframe caught fire.

"Veronica!" Thane called from across the room, holding out his hand.

I waved him off and threw myself even farther away from him and Jessa, avoiding another frost attack. Shards of ice and drywall shattered around me as the spell crashed against the wall. "Get her to safety. I'll meet you there."

A look of indecision crossed his face before he pressed his lips together and nodded. A second later, they were gone.

I glanced around the room for the first time, dread settling over my shoulders, almost weighing me down. The only exit was the one I came in through. I was in a motherfucking windowless storage room in the middle of the school building.

As another blast of cold air flew into the room, I dove behind a stack of student desks.

"Ms. Neill, I do believe I have you alone and cornered," drawled William's voice from outside the door. Fitting that his Winter Court magic was pure frost.

"Oh, no, whatever shall I do?" As bold as my words sounded, I was wracking my brain trying to figure a way out of this mess. The fae mage knew I could shift into bird form, so he was likely expecting me to do just that, which meant I needed to come up with a new solution. I urged the flames at the door to build until it was impenetrable without causing serious burns.

"I have no intention of harming you unless I have to." His voice hardened at my taunt. "But you have something I need."

"Are you even more delusional than I thought, Bill?" I threw back, my gaze still sweeping the area for an out. My pulse thudded in my ears as fear trickled through my body. I might have been trapped, which meant fighting my way out through who-knew-how many mages. "You just tried to frost me."

A malicious chuckle drifted into the room. "Only to pin you down. What was it the vampire liked to call you? Little bird?"

"Can't come up with your own nicknames, you have to steal a dead man's?"

But as he used the nickname from Xavier, my gaze settled on a vent in the ceiling. I was small enough to fit through the air conditioning tunnels and faster while in falcon form than the fae man. I just needed to get the vent off the ceiling and get in there before William realized what I was doing.

"Let's not make this more difficult by hurling insults." He clucked his tongue. "Come on out."

I grabbed the Dagger of Abaddon, slipped it into one of my empty sheaths, and gripped the legs of the desk I leaned against. I urged my fire into it, heating the metal. "See, the problem is if I come out there, I'm going to have to kill you."

Another chuckle. "I welcome the attempt."

The heat continued to move up the stacked desks, the metal turning red-hot. It would leave a nasty burn. Just a little bit more. "What is it you need from me anyway?"

"It would be far more fun to show you."

"Angels aren't working out for you, huh?" The desks were molten and about to buckle and collapse. As much as I wanted to find out what he needed from me, it was time to fly before I became a birdie popsicle. "I guess I have no choice but to come out peacefully."

With a big heave and the help of a fiery blast, I sent the

desks skidding across the floor toward the door. An inferno erupted at the door as the desks toppled outward, and shouts of surprise and pain rang out in the hallway. I had my fingers crossed they actually expected me to come out next.

Instead, I created another whip from my fire and snapped it toward the vent. The end curled around a slat, pulling the whole thing to the floor. After a quick shift into bird form, I swooped up into the tunnel, using my avian senses to lead the way to open air.

William's screech of fury echoed behind me, followed by icicles ricocheting off the metal walls of the tunnel until they crashed and shattered. Cold wind nipped at my tail feathers, but he was too late.

I was gone.

CHAPTER 16

Thursday Afternoon

I flew straight to the agency headquarters and landed on Adam's balcony. After shifting back into human form, I tapped on the sliding door. My heart beat rapidly, and I took deep breaths of the salty ocean breeze to slow my racing pulse. The archangel was on the phone at his desk, but when he caught sight of me behind the glass, he ended the call. The door slid open a moment later.

"How is she?" I asked as I stepped inside, shutting the door behind me.

"Thanks to you and Agent Munro's quick work, she will live."

"And her wing?"

Sighing, he moved back behind the desk but didn't sit. His wings fluttered as he glanced down at his papers. "That is to be determined. They cut through bone with one of their Daggers. Time will tell if they fuse together again properly. Healing with magic can only do so much, even divine healing."

I slumped into a chair even though it wasn't offered, letting out a whoosh of breath. My hands trembled as the drain from shifting caught up to me, but I forced myself to draw the Dagger that might have disabled my guardian angel forever and set it on Adam's desk. Only one more to go. "This is the one they used. What will happen to her if she can't fly again?"

Adam glanced sharply at me even as he picked up the blade. "We do not discard our angels like trash, if that is your concern."

I flinched at the harshness of his voice. Discarding was most definitely not what I meant, unless we were talking about Sophia, the reaper who cheated her way to angel wings. Then by all means. "No, I—"

"She will be brought back to full health and resume her healing duties." He took a deep breath and pinched the bridge of his nose with his free hand. "My apologies for my poor tone, Ms. Neill. Times have been difficult."

"Why don't you call your higher-ups for help? What about your god?"

"As with your own creators, the Almighty has given each of us a purpose and a fate." Adam turned the knife over in his hands. "No amount of prayers will change that."

"Okay, well, there must be angels above you who can bring in reinforcements, especially if they know these

Daggers are involved."

The archangel's gaze met mine. "If I cannot keep my city safe, then I will be removed from my seat of power."

I raised an eyebrow. "No offense, Adam, but I think you need to set your pride aside on this one. Surely we can argue on your behalf after this is all over if it means having backup now."

"My replacement will not treat you as fairly or kindly as I have, Ms. Neill. And he or she will likely desire to have a much stronger presence in your life." He dropped his gaze back to the Dagger. "The phoenix species needs to continue sooner rather than later."

My body went numb with shock. Was he saying what I thought he was? And I thought hearing it from a vampire was bad. "They can't do that. And why should it matter to you guys whether the phoenix goes extinct or not?"

"They can, and they will. They will force you to obey, and they will choose someone for you if necessary." His eyes met mine, the bright blue still dimmed to navy. "And we both know it will not be Agent Munro. Even if it were physically possible, he is very close to earning his wings."

Someone must have punched me in the gut. Or ripped out my heart and hurled it onto the floor. Everything inside me hurt, as if my own fast-acting poison had ripped its way through my veins. If Thane was that close to getting his angel wings, it meant he was closer to being out of my reach forever than I thought. Angels might seem human, but all their animalistic and carnal impulses were gone. The only things that remained were mere memories or shadows of their human emotions.

"How close?" My voice barely squeaked out of my

tightened throat.

"Any day now." He set the knife down on his desk.

My world spun as dizziness took hold. I knew Thane was getting up there in the ranks, but I had no idea he was *that* close. Why the hell didn't he tell me? And why was he jeopardizing it with all the sexy time with me, for fuck's sake? He was supposed to be proving his goodness, his holiness. I leaned forward, elbows on my knees, afraid I might vomit. Getting laid in the afterlife wasn't worth risking your wings and being thrown into the fiery pits.

If he wouldn't put an end to our little…whatever we were, I would.

Adam didn't answer my question about why they wouldn't let my species go extinct, but to be honest, I didn't really care anymore. What I did care about was why and how they thought coercing me to make babies with a mate of their choice was in any way, shape, or form acceptable. I bit the inside of my cheek and sat straight again. "How in your god's name is forcing me to do your bidding considered angelic? Especially when it comes to who and when I fuck?"

He sighed. "Our history is rife with moments of asking followers to do the unthinkable."

"My gods will never allow this." I gripped the arms of the chair.

"In the human realm, they have no choice."

A lightbulb sparked to life in my brain. "*Mirognya.*"

Adam stilled, his entire body tensing as if prepared to fight or flee.

"You know what it is," I accused, rising to my feet to be closer to eye level with him. "Is it the phoenix realm? Is that a thing?"

"Where did you hear that word?"

"This might sound crazy, but a stag told me in the woods."

Adam stared at me.

"In the Otherworld," I added.

He drew in a sharp breath, his eyes widening. "You spoke to the Keeper of the Forest?"

"Blacker than midnight coat? Eyes like starlight?"

Adam's nod was nearly imperceptible.

"Then, yep. I guess so."

"He has not been seen in a thousand years." His tone was wistful.

"Bummer you didn't get an invite." I allowed frustration to taint my tone. "But let's get back to *Mirognya*."

"Now is not the time to explain." Adam returned to his stern voice. "We are in the midst of a war with the necromancers. When the dust has settled, I will discuss *Mirognya* with you."

I gaped at him. "You can't possibly expect me to just drop this right now."

"I am not asking, Ms. Neill. I will tell you everything you need to know—*after* the necromancers have been put down."

Staring at the desk between us, I grappled internally, unsure how to handle the situation. I wanted to punch my fist through a wall or a face. He was completely right that now wasn't a *good* time, but would there ever really be a good time with the way things were going? I also didn't know enough about Adam and what buttons I could push. I would need to do some serious digging when this was all over, so I would be prepared when the next time occurred.

"I will drop this for now if you answer a question about the mages." I looked up to find him gazing at me. He nodded. "Why are the necromancers after me?"

"What could be more tempting to a master of Raising the dead than a phoenix whose magic is pure resurrection?"

I blinked. "He wants to harness my magic to create Risen?"

"With your magic, he could Raise entire battlefields in one go."

My mouth parted as the horror of that imagery settled in. Before I could respond, the door opened and Thane let himself in.

"Any change?" Adam asked.

Thane approached the desk and stood beside me. The muscles along his neck twitched as he clenched his teeth. "The healer put her into a resting coma so her body can heal. He thinks the wing will reattach without trouble."

I sighed in relief. Even though Jessa would be able to continue to work without the limb, having it functional would make her job far easier. An angel with a broken wing was such a tragic thought.

Thane's eyes focused on me, narrowing dangerously. "Was it William?"

I nodded and explained how I escaped and what the asshole necromancer said.

"That was way too close." He ran a hand through his dark hair. "We can't afford to let him get his hands on your magic."

"He won't," I said. "He's not as clever as he thinks he is."

"Sooner or later, he'll catch on to your limitations," he

warned. "You need to stay here or at your penthouse from now on."

I huffed. "I'm more than capable of taking care of myself, as I just proved."

"Veronica, you don't need to prove your strength to us." Thane took my hands in his, stroking the backs with his thumbs. "We already know you're more than capable of fighting, and fighting well. But that doesn't mean you're invincible."

I bit my lip, partly because he was right, but also because the heat of his touch brought back intense memories of our time together the night before...as well as the sudden realization that I would never be able to return the favor. There was no way I would let him risk his wings on time spent with me, no matter how much my body screamed otherwise.

"I'm not going to hide away every time some idiot with an agenda comes after me." I gave his hands a squeeze before releasing them. "William won't be the last, I'm sure of it."

Adam crossed his arms. "You may be right, but that does not mean we cannot take every precaution. I will provide you with two guards."

"While I appreciate the gesture, I don't plan on being followed around day and night," I said. "Besides, the last thing we need is even more dead or maimed angels."

"I planned to assign reapers," he said.

Before I could argue again, the door opened and a reaper stuck his head in. "My apologies, Archangel, but the Risen are on the move."

CHAPTER 17

Thursday Evening

When the reaper said Risen were on the move, I didn't think he meant *this* many of the walking dead for fuck's sake. The streets and alleys around the Brickell City Centre were crawling with them, sending humans running and screaming in all directions. It was fucking chaos, and it was going to be a nightmare to clean up. Even worse once the human police arrived, or if any news vans or helicopters showed up before that.

No time to think about any of that just yet. First, we needed to stop them.

Thane and a group of reapers would head for the main horde, taking them down from the inside out using their teleportation devices. One squadron of angels would provide surveillance from the sky and use their magic to cloak the Risen and the fight from human eyes as much as they could. Another unit would start at the infestation's edges, picking off stragglers, and a third would track down any human witnesses. Adam also sent a handful of reapers to alert the hospital staff and police chief who already knew about the Community's existence.

Like I said, a fucking mess.

I volunteered to be part of the second sky patrol, joining those fighting on the edges and working our way in. More than one member of the DEA tried to convince me to stay with the surveillance crew, but I wasn't made for watching— I was made for kicking ass. Besides, the angels could communicate with each other telepathically, and I'd just have my regular falcon screech. Not super helpful in this scenario.

In the fading evening light, I swooped down along the outer edges of the horde, ready to fight my way in and keep them from spreading any further. I landed next to a shuffling skeleton and shifted into human form, cutting the Risen down with one of my knives. The stench of decay permeated the air so thick it was almost tangible. Wait, no. It was definitely tangible. I gagged into my forearm, tasting the rot on my tongue. This was going to be rough.

I wished I'd had time to suit up properly. Lisa, the short sword I named after the Russian word for she-fox, hadn't seen any love since I faced William's first army of undead in the stadium. I winced, realizing I hadn't even checked on her since I got back from exile. No guns, either. For now, my knives would have to do the trick. I never went anywhere without at least a few easy-to-hide blades.

Two reapers appeared next to me, stepping out of teleportation circles and activating their scythes. I rolled my eyes. Despite my best arguments, Adam sent them to protect me, of course. I'd handle that problem later.

I slammed one of my knives into a Risen's temple until it sank into squish, nudging the body off the blade to collapse on the ground as soon as the reanimated light snuffed from its eyes. It didn't take much to stop a Risen—just a deep hit to the brain, decapitation, or fire. The problem with these guys was the volume. And if William unleashed any of his shifters, things would get real ugly, real quick.

With the reapers working alongside me, we took down the Risen outliers, moving slowly but surely toward the main horde and the reapers fighting there. No-longer-walking bodies were strewn across the road and sidewalk behind us, and more Risen kept coming. I panted and brushed strands of damp hair off my face. I didn't know if it was sweat or blood—probably a hearty mix of both. The smell had abated somewhat, but that likely meant I had just grown used to it. I scrunched up my nose. Ugh.

Because my attention was on the fight right in front of me, I didn't notice we were surrounded until it was too late. Things went downhill fast—there were just too many of the reanimated dead, even for my reaper bodyguards. I swung, my blade connecting with another temple; the Risen dropped, and another took its place. The muscles of my arms and legs burned as I ducked and thrust again.

Bony hands grabbed my shoulder, pulling me off-balance. When I tried to right myself, I slipped in a puddle of blood and went down. Rolling quickly before I became the bottom of an undead dog pile, I came face-to-face with unseeing dead eyes—a human woman who hadn't gotten lucky running away. I scrambled back, my heart in my throat, and let one of the reapers help me to my feet before a few sets of hands pulled him away.

Adam might have warned me not to use my magic on the streets, but I had enough of this bullshit. Time to light these fuckers up.

A whoosh of air brought my attention up for a moment, just in time to see a shadowy figure land in a crouch on the top of a nearby car. Glowing yellow eyes peered out from beneath the hood, staring right at me—the same figure as after the car accident.

I narrowed my eyes in return, unsure of this person's intent. Were they there to attack me this time? Collect the bounty on my head? Was this entire horde a distraction?

The figure performed an acrobatic flip off the car, cloak flaring out into the sky, and joined the fight against the Risen.

I blinked. Sun and flames. They were fighting on *our* side?

A dead man's teeth sank into my arm. I yelled and slammed my other knife into the back of his head. The reanimation magic fled, but his teeth stayed attached to my arm as others moved in closer. A flutter of fear tickled my heart. Fighting with a dead man stuck to my arm was going to be a serious hindrance.

Fuck. I shoved a blade into the gap between his teeth and used it as a crowbar. The teeth pulled loose, along with a chunk of my skin. I grimaced and turned back to the fight, knowing the wound would heal soon.

Somewhere on the other side of the group of dead attacking us, pops of bright magic lit up the pink and orange sunset sky as mages dueled with reapers and angels. The briefest moment of relief passed through me, knowing I wouldn't have anything to do with street cleanup or reconfiguring human memories. With backup moving closer and a new ally in the mix, I took the Risen down one by one, catching glimpses of the whirling dervish that was the cloaked figure. He—or possibly she?—moved with the grace and ease of an experienced fighter. My curiosity was beyond piqued.

As the figure leaned back to kick a body away, the cloak's hood slipped back enough for me to tell it was a man with red hair. Still holding a glow, though lighter without the hood's shadows, his eyes met my curious gaze. Then he ducked beneath reaching skeletal arms to tumble away.

The memory finally clicked into place. He had been in the parking garage after the agency was attacked by Risen, before I had my little adventure in Tucson. This guy had been following me for a long time. I frowned. Was he a bounty hunter?

No, that didn't make sense—he could have taken me hostage on more than one occasion by now. His skills were superior to mine, even I could admit that.

I wasn't the only one keeping my eye on him. The two reapers who joined me in the fight closed in on him as we neared the bigger group of reapers, where most of the Risen were officially dead—but he was more than prepared for their attempted capture. Using a nearby car and restaurant awning, he flipped himself onto the roof in the blink of an eye. The king of moves a parkour pro would be jealous of.

"Wait!" I yelled after him.

The hooded figure paused on his perch, casting his glowing gaze back down at me for just a moment. He nodded, then he was gone.

I put my arms over my head and panted, my mouth drier than the desert—and I would know—as I looked around at the carnage. Partially decaying bodies and parts lay strewn across the asphalt and cement. A handful of mages lay among them, and the majority of the living were placed into a reaper sleeper coma. As far as I could tell, no reapers had fallen.

I found Thane standing near a group of sleeping mages. "Who the hell was that guy?"

The mages looked so peaceful I wanted to kick them in the face. Instead, I wiped off my blades on a somewhat dry spot of my pants before tucking them back into their sheaths.

"I was hoping you could tell me." Thane typed something out on his cell phone. "Cleaning crew is on its way."

"I've seen him before, at the car crash," I said just as the air thinned, announcing the impending arrival of a group of fresh reapers. Damn, they were fast.

Within minutes, the newcomers assessed the situation and whisked away all evidence of a supernatural fight, including the mages. Some things couldn't be hidden without more energy, like the dents made in the cars or the chunks of cement missing from sidewalks and walls. Not to mention all the broken glass from the windows. Another crew would come by soon to do a more thorough cleaning, and the witches and warlocks working with the DEA would wipe any human memories. The Community operated together to keep our existence a secret.

One of my throwing knives lay beside a car, half-hidden in the shadows. I bent to pick it up, and a flash of reddish-orange caught my eye beside a tire—a feather.

I slipped my knife back into its sheath and ran the feather between my fingers. At first glance, it looked like one of mine in falcon form, only this one made my fingers tingle with magic. This wasn't an ordinary falcon feather…

…it was from a phoenix.

Holy. Flaming. Shit.

CHAPTER 18

Thursday Evening

A phoenix feather." Kit raised a disbelieving eyebrow. She must have thought I was crazy, which might not have been too far off the mark these days. Just not about this. "How can you be sure?"

After a quick check-in at the DEA, Thane and I teleported to her apartment. As had almost become normal now, the headquarters was a hot mess while Adam organized various task forces to clean up the chaos the Risen and necromancers created on the streets of Miami. The archangel had already brushed me off once about my species and the possibility of a phoenix realm, so I nudged Thane out of Adam's office when no one was looking.

If Kit couldn't help us, we would go back to Adam and force some answers out of him. Because forcing answers out of an archangel would be so easy.

One problem at a time. The good news was Angela wasn't here. As much as I wanted to get to know her, it was probably for the best since I wasn't handling this situation super well.

"If I could explain how I know any better, I would," I snapped. I understood Kit and Thane's matching states of disbelief, but that didn't make it any less frustrating. Turning toward the reaper, I snapped my fingers as a new thought came to me. "It's like how I knew the Risen at the morgue was a shifter."

When the Risen had first started popping up well over a month ago, I ran into one on the shoreline at Alice Wainwright Park. Literally. I went for a run to let off some steam, and a decaying body ambled right past me. Later on at the morgue, I was able to tell that the guy was a shifter. Only I still had no idea how I knew that fact simply by being in his presence and others didn't.

Another problem for another day. The list of future problems was starting to get long. Magical stuff always created a whole new level of fun to my life.

Fun being subjective, of course.

Thane nodded slowly. "I remember. You sensed he wasn't a human."

"Right," I said, excited that he was finally getting it. "I don't know what kind of ability allows me to sense the supernatural, but the same thing is happening with the feather."

Kit turned the feather over in her hands. "There's a

spell that can help track down the owner."

"Is that an offer from you?" I asked.

"No, I would ask Luciana Perez. She's the most powerful witch still active in the Miami coven, she'll get you the closest." She met my gaze. "She'll want something in return."

I waved a hand dismissively. "Money won't be a problem. You know that."

"She won't want your money and will be offended if you offer it. She'll want something personal."

My eyebrows drew together. "Like what?"

She shrugged as she handed the feather back. "Could be as simple as a favor or a strand of your hair, though I advise against giving her anything that carries your DNA."

I groaned. "Great. What if she won't do it? Or won't accept anything except my hair?"

"She'll do it. Just be cautious, and don't be afraid to negotiate."

Luciana's shop, The Witch's Brew, was located in the heart of *el Mercado Sombra,* the Shadow Market that acted as a sanctuary for the Community. The store was just as cluttered and chaotic as the last time we visited. When we entered, pungent smells from various herbs and potions assaulted my nose, which wrinkled in response. Crystals of all shapes and sizes and every hue imaginable were scattered across shelves or tossed in baskets, next to relics, animal charms, and miniature statues of various deities.

I hadn't expected a reorganization of the store, and it

really wasn't all that long since we were here before anyway. Perhaps Luciana kept it this way to appeal to more frugal shoppers who couldn't afford fancier stores where the shelves were practically barren, although the price tags here ranged from mere pennies to astronomical figures. One tag attached to a jar of pitch-black liquid even read, "Ask owner for price." I shuddered to even think of what it contained.

The witch stood behind the counter, wrapping up some items for the current customer. Her ink-black hair fell around her shoulders in waves the ocean would cry over. She smiled as she handed the paper bag to the woman, who gave us a quick, curious glance before she left.

"So we meet again," Luciana said. Her bronzed skin was free of wrinkles or lines, making her appear much younger than she actually was. Mere decades old rather than centuries. Power drifted off her, rippling through the air to dance around us. Her dark gaze met mine. "The last phoenix and a grim reaper. Life and death. A fitting partnership, is it not?"

The way she said *partnership* held a deeper meaning than just two people working together for the agency. It was like she knew we had become closer on an intimate level. I wasn't really surprised, but that damn sense of destiny flared up inside me again, the one that kept telling me Thane's life was bound to mine in some inexplicable way. Except now I needed to let him go. A shiver shook my shoulders, and I scratched at my chest.

"I need to request your services locating the person who this belongs to." I withdrew the feather from my bag and placed it on the counter.

Her dark brown eyes widened. She hovered her fingers over the feather, caressing without ever touching it. "A phoenix feather, but not one of yours." She glanced up at me for confirmation.

I nodded and dug my elbow into Thane's side, earning a grunt. Once again, my unknown ability or gut instinct had been right.

"Yes, I can help you track the owner down." Luciana withdrew her hand reluctantly. "It will cost you, of course."

I nodded again. "What will you accept as payment?"

Her eyes moved between me and the reaper before settling back on me. "A story."

I raised an eyebrow. Not what I was expecting. "Excuse me?"

"I would like you to tell me one of the stories your mother told you as a little girl when she tucked you in at night."

A bedtime story? I was sure I misunderstood. "I'm confused. The price for the spell is just a story? Like, right now?"

She smiled and leaned her elbows on the counter, clasping her hands in front of her. Dark hair tumbled down around her shoulders and arms, sending out the scent of cinnamon and rain. "Right now."

I pursed my lips and racked my brain. It had been years since I thought about those stories. Now I needed to pull out one of my long-forgotten memories on the fly—or out of my ass. Maybe both, but I had a feeling she would know if it was out of my ass. Damn it.

"Okay, long ago and far away, in a kingdom made of fire and glass, lived a princess and a prince," I began, tendrils of memories finding their way to the forefront of my mind. "They were very happy, with a mother and father who loved them more than anything else in the world. Most of the kingdom loved them as well, for they were special children, born from two pure royal lines that could be traced back for millennia. As a matriarchal kingdom, the princess would inherit everything upon her mother's death."

The more I spoke, the more the memories came back. My mother's lilting voice and adoring face as she sat beside my bed at night flooded through my mind, and my heart ached in response.

"But not everyone loved them. There was an evil sorceress who wanted the throne for herself and would do anything in her power to take it. She spread evil thoughts and rumors amongst the people, claiming the time had come for the current royal line to be replaced. She raised an army to attack the palace and kill the royal family.

"Only when the invaders searched the palace, the family was nowhere to be found. The evil sorceress called for a great hunt, promising riches and titles beyond compare for anyone who could locate the prince and princess. But day after day, month after month, year after year, they failed. And soon the sorceress grew complacent, assuming the prince and princess must have died. No one could hide from her dark power for so long.

"But one day, the prince and princess will return and take back the throne that is their birthright, and the evil sorceress will fall. Good will always prevail over evil, no matter how dark the path may seem."

CHAPTER 19

Thursday Evening

I was sure I missed a detail here or there in my mother's bedtime story, but I was pretty damn proud of myself for remembering as much as I did. I couldn't even think of the last time she had told it.

Luciana smiled at me, a weird, knowing look on her face. "Beautiful. Thank you."

"My mom loved to tell fairy tales like that," I said. "But was that really all you wanted as payment?"

"That's it." The witch reached beneath the counter and pulled out some bottles and jars. "You know, bedtime stories often have some truth in them."

Don't tell that to Hansel and Gretel.

"How does the spell work?" I asked, instantly intrigued as she opened one of the jars and sprinkled a dash of a powdery grey substance like ashes along the feather. I really wished Kit still practiced magic so I could learn some of this from her.

Luciana lit a stick of incense, blowing on it softly to fuel the ember, then waved the smoke over the feather too. "The ash and smoke will draw the essence of the phoenix out of the feather. When I chant the incantation, I'll know where he or she is at the current moment. You will need to get there quickly if you hope to catch up to them." She glanced at us. "Are you ready?"

Thane withdrew his t-port device and held my hand in the other. Warmth spread along my limbs, down to my toes; my body wanted to meld itself to him and never let go. Ending things with him was going to be so fucking hard. That heat was irresistible.

An itch flared up again at a spot below my left breastbone, and I gave it a good scratch.

Luciana chanted in a deep voice, too low for me to understand the words even if they were English, which I doubted. The feather rose off the counter, following the witch's hands while she worked her magic. An orange incandescent light grew around it as it circled in the air, and when she moved her hands toward herself, the glow detached from the feather, which dropped back to the counter.

The orange light drifted toward the witch, and she waved it into her face, closing her eyes and breathing in deep. Orange sparkles encompassed her face like a veil, then soaked into her skin. When she opened her eyes again, a dim sunset hue glowed briefly behind her irises.

Luciana tilted her head to the side, her eyes unfocused, and chuckled. "Ah, of course."

I raised an eyebrow as she handed me the feather.

"You teleported here from Ms. Parker's place, yes?" She smiled when my bewildered look confirmed her question. "He waits for you there, on a rooftop. He cannot follow the reaper's mode of travel. Go, quickly."

"Wait, he's still following me?" Before I had time to process what that meant or how she had known the phoenix was a male, Thane activated his device and the world dropped out beneath us.

When I felt solid ground under my feet again, I opened my eyes and saw darkness. Had we gotten stuck in some sort of teleporting limbo? My heart raced until the city's twinkling lights caught my attention. We were on a flat roof—Kit's roof, to be exact. Ignoring the light nausea rolling in my belly, I pushed away from Thane to quickly scan the other rooftops.

There. A hand leaning on the edge of the roof next door, white skin shining like a beacon in the streetlights and disappearing beneath the figure's long sleeves. As soon as I spotted him, he glanced up, eyes emitting that same unnatural glow as they settled on me. He turned and sprinted in the opposite direction.

"Wait!" I yelled, frustration gripping my word. This was getting a bit repetitive for my taste. Just as I considered shifting into my bird form to follow him, he swirled his cloak around himself and...

...disappeared? How the fuck was that even possible?

I shifted into falcon form anyway and swooped over the roofs, trying to spot him, but he had vanished into thin air. Did he have magic that I didn't? I landed beside Thane and shifted back to human form, stomping angrily across the rooftop and back. When I stopped, Thane regarded me with a smirk.

"Don't judge me," I huffed. Sure, stomping was a tad dramatic for anyone, let alone a grown ass woman, but it also got some of my frustration out. "Are you coming back to Kit's with me?"

"Yes, but first..." Thane reached out and caught my hand, drawing me into his chest before I could resist. His other hand went behind my neck and pulled my lips to his.

The kiss was ravenous, his tongue consuming my mouth and breath like a starving man. He tasted like ocean air, of salt-filled breezes warmed by sunshine. I moved up onto my tiptoes, wrapping my arms around his neck, trying to get as close as possible to this man who made my insides melt and my heart sing. His hands moved down to my waist, then slid up the inside of my shirt, his thumbs slipping beneath my bra to caress the sides of my breasts.

To hell with letting him go. This man was mine. I moaned into his mouth, every inch of my body tingling and throbbing with desire and need.

Then the motherfucker pulled away. I glared at him, bewildered as I panted into the warm night air. The only satisfaction was the fact that he was also out of breath and very obviously aroused by our little rooftop make out session. That or he stuffed a nicely sized banana in his pants when I wasn't looking.

Thane ran a hand through his tousled hair, courtesy of yours truly, and let out an amused breath. "You have no idea what you're doing to me."

I laughed and drew up close to him again, pressing my palms to his chest. "Oh, I definitely have an idea."

I ran my hands over his stomach through his shirt, over those rock-hard abs I could wash laundry on, and let them drift downward. The back of my hand brushed over the hardness hidden inside his pants, earning a groan from him. His gaze drilled deep into mine as I slipped my hands into his pockets. Distracting him with my fingers doing dirty things inside his pants, he didn't notice me activating his t-port device until we were pulled away from the roof and found ourselves back at Kit's place.

As my best friend glanced up at us from her desk, Thane pressed his lips together and narrowed his eyes at me. "I'll be back in a moment." He all but slammed the bathroom door behind him, rattling the picture frames along the wall.

I snickered. Served him right for thinking he could leave me smoldering after that kiss. But also, hurray for me and my ability to stop things from going further. I made myself at home in Kit's kitchen and opened up the freezer, meeting her knowing gaze as I grabbed a handful of ice from the bucket and tossed them down my shirt.

"You guys have got to bone already," she said.

I let out a deep sigh as the ice melted and did its job to get my fire back under control. The heat of my inner flame dried the wet spot on my shirt. "Not going to happen."

She tsked. "You're delusional."

"I'll explain later." My shoulders drooped, and I leaned against the fridge. He better get his wings soon—my impulse control was terrible.

"No luck with Luciana?" She knew not to push for details. I would offer them willingly when I could.

"Oh, we had luck," I said just as the bathroom door opened and Thane reappeared. He unbuttoned his shirt a few extra buttons, and water dripped down from his hair. Catching my mouth hanging open at the delicious sight, I snapped it shut and focused on explaining to Kit what had happened on the rooftop.

She leaned her chin on her palm, her elbow resting on the desk. "Great, so now my place is being watched by some unknown entity?"

"That was probably true even before this guy showed up. I just want to know who he is and why he's following me."

She rolled her eyes. "That's far from all you want to know."

"True. I have so many questions."

"No wonder he's avoiding you."

I gave her the middle finger. "Anyway, now what? Adam isn't going to tell me shit about anything until this whole potential zombie apocalypse is over. William picked the *worst* time to throw a hissy fit."

Thane's smirk made an appearance. "I'm sure he did it on purpose, just to get under your skin."

"Don't you two gang up on me."

"Us? Never." Kit almost managed to look innocent. Almost.

I glanced back and forth between them with narrowed eyes. This was what I got for being banned from Miami for a month. A mere four weeks and these two developed some inside jokes.

Thane's phone beeped. He glanced at the face of the smartwatch, then back up at me. "The wolves found the necromancers."

CHAPTER 20

Thursday Night

I pushed myself off Kit's fridge "Where?"

"Adam didn't say." Thane pulled out his teleportation device. "But he wants everyone to meet at the DEA building for a briefing."

I turned to Kit. "Come with us. You may know something magic-related that can help stop William."

She eyed the cylindrical object in the reaper's hand. "Fine, but I'll drive myself. I don't want to be reliant on the reapers to get back here."

Thane reached out to me, but I shook my head. "I'll fly back so I can keep an eye on her."

He frowned. "I don't think you should be flying solo right now."

"I need to talk to Kit." I crossed my arms. "Alone."

She raised her eyebrows in my direction but didn't say anything.

Thane looked like he was going to argue again but thought better of it. "Just be safe." He pressed a kiss to my forehead and stepped into the teleportation circle.

"Can we talk and walk on the way to my bike?" Kit asked. "I don't like the idea of you being without protection for too long, either."

"Let's go." I followed her out the door and down the hall to the elevator.

When the doors closed us inside, she pushed the button for the lobby. "Okay, spill."

I pulled down the top of my shirt to show her the red mark on the left side of my chest, above my bra. "Any idea what this is?"

"Girl, I'm not a doctor." Still, she leaned in close to take a look. "Is that a hickey?"

I muttered and pulled my shirt back up. "No, it's not. But it showed up this morning after Thane and I had a moment together last night."

She stared at me. "I thought you said you hadn't slept with him yet?"

"I haven't. Not fully, anyway. He took care of my needs, and that was it." I rubbed at the spot beneath my shirt. "But I noticed when he kissed me on the roof just now that it itched. Come to think of it, it's itched a few times today."

"No wonder you needed ice."

"Right, except Adam told me Thane's close to earning

his wings," I said. "Like, any day now."

Kit's eyes widened. "Well, shit. Talk about poor timing."

The door to the elevator opened, and the sound of crackling electricity filled my ears.

The world went black as I passed out.

Fuck, my head hurt. I held a hand to my temple, as if that would somehow ease the throb, and used the other to push myself up to sitting. The floor was cold beneath my palm and legs, the chill seeping deep into my bones. I had been out for a while. Also, where the fuck was I?

Darkness enclosed the area, wherever I was, so I activated my ability to sense heat signatures. Metal bars surrounded me on four sides, welded into a metal base and matching top—a cage. My breath hitched in my throat, and my body temperature dropped even lower.

I was in a motherfucking *cage*.

I patted my pockets only to find them empty of my cell phone. A quick glance around showed someone took my purse, too. A figure lay with their back to me, and it took me a second to recognize the dark braids and ripped jeans.

"Kit!" I crawled over on hands and knees, ignoring the pounding in my head as the movement rattled my brains against my skull. They—whoever that was—had definitely done something extra to knock me the fuck out so well.

She stirred as I reached her, groaning when she raised a hand to her head, too. "Am I hungover?"

"I wish." I helped her sit up and ignited a small flame in the palm of my hand, holding it out so she could see our surroundings. "Looks like we've been kidnapped, and I think drugged."

Her gaze swept the bars and top of the cage. There was no door, which meant they welded us inside while we were knocked out. "Bounty hunters or the Society?"

"I don't know yet."

"Can you melt the bars?"

I grasped a bar in my free hand and pushed my fire into it. The metal tingled beneath my palms but didn't respond to my magic, which wasn't a big surprise. "Must be coated with some sort of magical fire retardant."

A door opened on our left, allowing light to flood the room from outside. I extinguished my flame and squinted against the sudden brightness, holding a hand over my eyes. With a click of a switch, an overhead fluorescent glare bathed the room and three masked figures entered—only I realized it wasn't a room. We were in a cage inside a box truck.

Judging by the figures' shapes and clothing, they were all men. Each mask could have come from a Halloween store, featuring various terror-inducing creatures—a snarling werewolf, a grotesque skull, and Jason. I would be willing to bet these men were the same masked assholes who crashed into and destroyed my car.

"Oh, look, the sleeping beauty has woken up," said the wolf, his white t-shirt stretched tight across a well-muscled chest.

I glanced at the other two. Yep, also fit. We'd have a good fight on our hands to get out of here.

"Shame," said Jason, his voice deep and gravelly. "I wanted to wake her with a kiss." He grabbed his crotch. "A kiss with my cock."

They all laughed, and I rolled my eyes. "Like no idiot has come up with that line before."

Although I couldn't see their eyes beneath the Halloween masks, I sensed the irritation as I spoiled their fun.

"I'd watch that tongue, phoenix," said the skull, his voice dark and deadly, "before I rip it from your throat." He approached the cage and crouched before me. "He only wants you *alive*."

I glared at him. His demeanor told me that he was the leader of the three and likely the deadliest of these hunters hoping to cash in on William's bounty. The tingle of awareness spread over me with his nearness, indicating a supernatural nature. All three must be Community members, and all three would be dead men when I got free.

The skull turned toward Kit. "And he didn't say anything about needing your friend."

I gripped the bar in front of me. "Touch her, and I promise your death will take a *very* long time."

The empty eye sockets returned to me, but it was impossible to tell what the man was feeling or thinking behind the mask. He stood. "Sit back and enjoy the ride, ladies. It'll be the first of many with us."

The three men laughed and jumped down out of the truck. Before closing us into the darkness again, Jason blew me a kiss. Fucker.

"Got any ideas?" I asked, turning to my best friend as I lit a flame in my palm again.

"You need to go nuclear and get to the agency," she said. The truck's engine rumbled as the vehicle started.

"You know I can't do that." I shook my head. "You wouldn't make it."

"They're probably thinking the same thing." She shrugged and looked me straight in the eye. "But I've lived long enough."

I glared at her as the truck began to move. "It's not an option. What else have you got?"

She closed her eyes and rested her head against the bars behind her. "Unless you have more magical secrets to confess, I'm out of ideas."

I watched my best friend for a moment, thinking through our predicament. The flickering flames in my hand cast moving shadows across her face. How many times had we thought through problems with each other over the last five years? I wasn't going to give up without a fight. "Hey, remember how we met?"

Her lips curled up into a smirk. "You were such a newb."

I scoffed, but she wasn't wrong. "I'm lucky you didn't laugh in my face and walk away."

"It was obvious you needed help." Her tone held the smile that didn't quite raise her lips a second time.

Needing help was a massive understatement. My parents prepared me to fight and flee, but most importantly, to avoid the Community like the plague. When I was out partying one night before Mad died, I bumped into Kit. More like I ran into her in an intoxicated stupor and recognized her otherness. Thankfully, she allowed my stupid drunk ass to ask a million questions while she helped me stumble home.

"Why *did* you help me? Why not just call me a cab and

go your own way?"

She opened her eyes, dark irises dancing in the dim light of my flame. With a sigh, she closed them again. "You were a broken-winged bird trying to fly. Call me a sucker, but I couldn't turn my back on that."

A fitting description for my life back then. I still felt a bit broken, but day by day, I was healing with Kit's help. Humanity needed her help, too.

She was going to get mad at my next suggestion, but it was the only other solution I had. "Kit."

"Mm?"

"You need to do it."

She cracked an eye open to peek at me. "Do what?"

"Use magic."

She let out a short laugh and closed her eye again. "No."

"We have two options: I blow this place to smithereens and kill you in the process, or you use magic again." I nearly lost my balance as the truck took a sharp turn. "It's pretty fucking simple."

Both her eyes snapped open this time. "It's not fucking *simple*, Veronica. I made a vow never to use magic again, and I don't break my vows."

I groaned. "You made a vow to yourself, damn it. I think you can learn to forgive yourself."

"You weren't there. You didn't see what they made us do." Her gaze grew distant. "The humans surrendered; their memories had been wiped. There was no need to kill them."

I scooted closer and pulled her into my arms. Stiff at first, she softened, allowing me to provide her this small comfort. I already knew the story, how the High Priests of the covens sent to clean up the fae outing in Italy after World

War II ordered a massacre. All the human men, women, and children who saw or heard of the fae were killed after the witches and warlocks removed their memories. Hundreds were murdered in cold blood.

And Kit helped.

She felt betrayed by her own kind, ordered to do the unthinkable, so she swore to never use magic again. But not using magic anymore didn't stop the nightmares and the cold sweats. Kit had come to love humankind, and killing them so senselessly almost made her lose her damn mind.

I kissed the top of her head, breathing in her calming floral scent. "If you die, who will fight for them? Who will protect them from people like William? Who will protect Angela? We need you, Katherine Parker. Angela needs you. We need every part of who you are, no matter how scary." I paused. "Actually, scary would be great right now."

Her body tensed for a moment before she pulled away to look me in the face. Her eyes narrowed, not in anger, but in thought. "Since when did you get so wise?"

"I had the best teacher."

"Damn right." She pursed her lips. "It's time to fight."

CHAPTER 21

Thursday Night

I grinned at Kit. "Fuck yes."

I hadn't known whether she would listen to me or not, and now I was super excited to see her work magic. It was something I'd wanted to witness since the night we met. I honestly didn't know the extent of her magical abilities, but it was time to find out, and who knew, maybe she was looking for a good excuse to start using again. I'd heckle her for not doing it at the stadium another time, when we weren't in the midst of a life or death situation.

Kit pulled a green gemstone attached to a thin gold chain from beneath her shirt. "We know the bounty hunters aren't from the witch Community—there's no way they would've left me with this."

"You've been ready to use magic all along," I accused her in a playful tone.

"Despite my suggestion for you to go nuclear earlier, I value my life just as much as anyone. I knew you wouldn't do it." She hesitated, a flicker of nervousness flitting across her face. "Besides, I think I'm going to ask Angela to marry me."

"What!" I might have squealed. Ever since we met five years ago, I had never heard Kit utter those words about another person. To say this was a big moment didn't do it justice.

"I know. It's ridiculous and way too soon." Kit's dark gaze lifted to meet mine. "But I'm fucking happy. She gives me something to live for."

I grinned. "Then let's get you out of here."

"Go hold onto something, it's going to get bumpy."

I didn't need to be told twice. I wrapped my arms around the closest bars and held them in my fists.

She bowed her head over the necklace, cupping the gem in her hands, and chanted. Her black braids fell forward like a beaded curtain hanging around her face. A greenish glow swirled out of the gem and crept up her arms, wrapping around her shoulders like an emerald shroud—earth magic. When the glow sank into her skin, her veins pulsed, pushing toward the surface like they wanted to escape. Her entire body glowed emerald for a brief moment. She dropped the gem, which fell back against her chest, then pressed her sparkling palms to the bottom of our cage, still chanting. The truck bucked and swerved and muffled shouts of confusion and warning came from the cab.

Then we were rolling.

At some point, I shut my eyes. Probably when my legs ended up over my head. I winced as my shoulder banged hard into the bars. When the truck settled back on its wheels again with a groan, I opened my eyes.

Still rocking a greenish hue, Kit stood at the front of the cage as if the vehicle's roll hadn't affected her in the least. She reached up to grasp two bars and pulled. Her muscles strained beneath her skin, and the glow rose to the surface again and rushed down her hands, twisting around the metal. With an angry creaking, the bars pulled apart, just wide enough for us to step through.

"Is this like some sort of Hulk magic?" I asked.

She glanced at me as we moved toward the door. "Since when do you know anything about comics?"

Leave it to the comic nerd to take me way too literally. "Oh good, I was right. He *is* the big, green one Mark Ruffalo played."

She paused with a hand on the latch and shook her head, resigned to her fate as my best friend forever. "Ready?"

I cracked my neck. They might have taken my knives, but they couldn't take what my momma gave me—muscles, speed, and a whole lot of anger issues. "Let's kick some ass."

In one swift flick of her hand, she had the truck's back door unlocked and pushed open. We jumped down to the grass and immediately headed for the cab doors—she went right, I went left. I didn't know where we were, but the two-lane road we were on wasn't busy, and the few cars who passed gave us a brief glance before moving on.

Good. One less thing to worry about.

Only two of our abductors were in the truck, neither one the Skull. Damn, I really hoped to have a word with that guy. And by word, I meant *make him bleed.* At least we still had the opportunity to teach the traitors in the wolf and Jason masks a lesson. Both men were dazed in the cab, blood dripping freely down their faces. When I yanked open the passenger side door, Jason snapped out of it and kicked. I grabbed his foot and pulled. He flew out of the truck and landed with a tumble in the grass.

After leaping to his feet, he rushed me with a snarl. I ducked beneath his arm, then reached between his legs to grab his balls through his pants. His squeal cut off when I twisted around and threw my other arm around his neck, securing him in a chokehold.

"Not so cocky now, are we?" I asked, squeezing his balls harder.

His body jerked as he tried to get away, but my other arm held him tight.

"I don't want to kill you, but I have absolutely no problem with it if you don't answer my questions, got it?" I asked, tightening my hold between his legs for emphasis. I actually did want to kill him, but he might not talk if I was honest.

He squeaked out a yes.

"Good. Who is the guy in the skull mask?"

"Rico. Leader of the Hollow Hounds."

Rogue shifter clans weren't very common because most animal shifter types belonged to families, packs, and herds.

Even the big cats and bears came together to form families, no matter how distant they roamed. But like any species, outliers existed. In our world, that meant those who challenged traditional hierarchy, had a difficult time obeying rules, or were cast out for egregious behavior. Somehow, they always seemed to find each other and formed their own band of misfits.

I didn't think rogue shifters were inherently bad people, but they could definitely be a nuisance. Like these guys proved to be on more than one occasion.

"Why aren't you obeying the Archangel's cease and desist?" I asked.

Jason let out a strangled laugh. "The mage is offering up a place in his court when he replaces the fae queen."

"My life for a title? Seriously?" Condescension dripped like tar from my mouth, thick and dark.

"Our shifting magic is supercharged in the fae realm, and the crazy mage is offering our clan an open invite," he said. "The Summer Court will be ours for the taking. Anything we want—jewels, the palace, women."

My nostrils flared. Ugh. William was offering up his own people just to get his hands on my magic. So despicable.

"He's also offered us a chance to go next." He licked his lips. "The mage'll be first of course, but then we get a shot between those long, pretty legs of yours."

His cock jumped near my hand, where I still gripped him through his pants. It tried to grow hard with his rising excitement. My lip curled in disgust, and I let go of his balls to secure my other arm around his neck. I tightened the hold.

His hands reached up to grasp at it, trying to pull me away. But I just gripped tighter, using both arms to cut off his oxygen supply. When he slumped against me, I dropped him. My limbs shook with fury and disbelief as I stared down at him.

What the fuck was wrong with these people?

I drew minor satisfaction when I saw blood seeping from his open mouth—the fucker's teeth had bitten through his lip when he hit the ground. I should just kill him now. It was bound to happen anyway.

A hand touched my shoulder, and I jumped and nearly punched Kit in the face.

"Shit." I held a hand to my heart. "Sorry, I'm having a freak-out moment."

Her eyebrows drew together. "What happened?"

I waved a hand at the unconscious man at my feet, explaining what he had said. As I finished, she drew back a foot and kicked him hard in the ribs. He was out cold, but he'd have a nasty bruise when he woke. Good.

Blood on her hands caught my attention. I grabbed them and turned them over, examining them for injuries. "Are you hurt?"

She snatched her hands back. "No."

I stared at her, waiting for more of an explanation.

She glanced back down at the guy at our feet, her gaze hardened and angry. "Only one of them needs to play messenger."

Goosebumps crawled up my arms. She was totally right, but the fierceness in her eyes was new. Did using her magic again wake something inside of Kit? Something dangerous?

CHAPTER 22

Thursday Night

We found our phones and purses in the cab of the truck, and I immediately dialed Thane. "Hey, long story, but we got kidnapped. No big deal. We took care of it, but can you come get us and send a cleanup crew?"

A moment of silence before he answered, "Fucking hell, Veronica. On my way."

I almost giggled as the line went dead. I was probably losing my mind a little bit. There was no time to tell Kit the reaper was coming—which in any other circumstance would sound terrifying—before he was here. His blue-eyed gaze surveyed the scene and settled on me.

"Never a dull moment with you." He took my hand, I took Kit's, and we were back in Adam's office.

Nausea came and went in a flash. Funny—you really did get used to the sensation of being drawn and quartered the more you teleported. "How was I supposed to know we'd be ambushed before we even got out of the elevator?"

"Which is exactly why I wanted you to come straight here with me." Thane crossed his arms over his broad chest.

"But then they would have gotten Kit and used her to bargain or something," I pointed out. "If you hadn't noticed, we escaped all by ourselves. I only called you to get us here faster."

Adam cleared his throat, and we all turned to look at him. "Care to fill me in?"

I quickly explained the incident with the bounty hunters, leaving out the part about Kit using magic again. She was quieter than usual, and judging by her furrowed brows and distant gaze, she was deep in her thoughts. I glanced at her when I finished, hoping she didn't regret her decision to bust us out using magic.

She stared out the door leading to the balcony. Her forehead was still marked with deep creases from how tightly her eyebrows pulled together. Worry gnawed at my insides.

"I am glad you are both safe," the archangel said. "Now, let us join the others and put an end to this madness."

By the time we arrived, the large conference room was packed full of reapers, angels, and wolves—oh my. Wait, witches and warlocks were here, too. Dark grey metal folding chairs took up most of the space, each seat occupied while those who got here too late or were likely too anxious to sit stood along the back and side walls.

Other than Xavier's sentencing, I had never seen so many Community members together in one room before. Looked like I was really bringing the Community together with my involvement. I held back the laugh that wanted to escape and cleared my throat as quietly as I could.

It was a good thing we knew exactly where William was holed up thanks to the wolves, or else I might have suspected he'd bomb the DEA building right about now. Kit and I stayed to the back, behind the last row of metal chairs, not wanting to draw attention to ourselves. Thane moved to the front by Adam. No one here would be after the bounty placed on my head courtesy of one fae necromancer, but that didn't mean I needed to announce myself.

Despite knowing where William and his cronies were, I had a hard time shaking an eerie sense of foreboding as I listened to the chatter. I rubbed at the goosebumps rising on my arms. Had the wolves found the Society too easily? Was that throwing me off somehow? I must have been spooked from the whole abduction incident earlier.

"As you are all aware," Adam's voice immediately silenced the room, "the threat from William Caomhánach has reached critical levels and must be contained. We have lost too many lives to his immoral behavior. Furthermore, he and his mages are defiling the dead, and they are threatening the hidden existence of the entire Community."

He tapped the large, clear glass display screen beside him that reminded me of whiteboards from my high school days. If those boards had been super high-tech and transparent, anyway. It came to life, showing us a detailed map of Miami. Magic enhanced the topography, showing Community members moving about, a variety of colors indicating the different species. Only the fanciest technology for the agency.

Of course, cloaking magic and trinkets would keep some of us hidden, which is why Adam needed to call in the wolves and the other Community leaders' help. Chances were Luka received some help from the witch and warlock covens to penetrate the cloaking magic William was sure to be using. Their canine noses were good, but magic was still better.

I chanced a glance at Kit to see how she was doing, but her eyes were laser-focused on Adam's map.

"This is where the Society of the Dead has set up their new base, after their last was… dismantled."

The minor pause wouldn't have been noticeable to most, but I hid my grin behind a hand and caught the twinge in Thane's cheek as he fought back a smirk.

Dismantled. I had all but collapsed the stadium with the bomb-like blast of my rebirth. Any cloaking magic the necromancer had on the building failed and exposed the destruction to human authorities. Word on the human street was a construction detonation gone wrong.

Adam gestured to a circled area on the map. Tapping on the glass brought the image in close, showing us a newly built hotel with construction barricades surrounding it. Some of the upper levels weren't fully completed yet, remaining mostly open to the elements behind plastic tarp barriers. A yellow crane loomed nearby, a sleeping monolith waiting to be woken.

"Thirty-four floors filled with mages, fae, and the Risen," Adam said, casting his stern gaze around the room to add to the severity of his words. "Should they catch wind of what we plan and release the horde on the city, all hell will break loose. At zero hundred hours, all forces will rendezvous at our forward staging location."

He tapped a spot on the map near the hotel but far enough away to avoid detection by any patrols. "From here, all ground forces will move in, establishing containment around the building. Be cognizant not to alert any of their patrols. Luka will lead ground troops and will assign more specific responsibilities after this meeting. But be in position prior to zero one hundred hours. At that time, we go in fast, we go in hard. Those with wings will come in from above, securing the highest levels and maintaining the high-ground. We will force the hostile forces to fight us uphill as we work our way down."

So diplomatic. I pressed my tongue to the roof of my mouth to keep a snarky comment in. Everyone would assume he just meant the angels as those with wings, but he definitely included me in that group.

No one needed to know that just yet. Surprises could be fun.

Moving his hand to different areas of the map, Adam continued, "Once the attack on the roof has commenced, Luka and the pack will come from all angles on the ground. After removing any hostiles outside, they will secure all doors and exits in the event anyone attempts to flee. The witches and warlocks will form a perimeter a few meters out, ready to disable anyone who makes it outside by means other than the doors.

"With containment set above and below, Thane will lead the reapers, teleporting inside to surprise them in the middle of their base. This should catch the mages off-guard and sow confusion among their communication, preventing them from massing force against either of the containment teams."

My breath caught in my throat as my gaze shifted to the reaper. Thane was the frontline and therefore more likely to be killed, especially given the mages still had one of the Daggers of Abaddon. He knew what he signed up for when he took the position as a grim reaper, accepting that he must earn his wings, but I sure as fuck didn't sign up for that. Hell, I didn't sign up for falling in love with a reaper at all, especially not one who was going to become an angel any day now. There was a very good chance he would have them right after this necromancer bullshit was cleaned up.

Stars danced in my vision, and I forced myself to breathe before I blacked out. Shit. Did I really fall in love with him? The wild thumping of my heart told me I did.

I scratched at the spot above my left boob like my heart itched. I had forgotten about the red mark again. Once this was all over, I'd talk to Luciana or Adam about it. Maybe I contracted a virus from the Risen or something. Ew. I crinkled my nose.

Luka rose from his seat near the front, his shirt stretched tight across the muscles of his broad back. That man was built to be an alpha. "And Lady Emilia? Where do the vampires come in?"

His angry expression made it clear he knew exactly what had transpired with the vampires, and a chorus of voices joined in, wanting answers.

"At this time, the Master Vampiress has exercised her right to maintain neutrality due to the Winter Court fae's involvement and the queen's silence," Adam explained calmly. "However, the vampires will be ready to catch any stragglers who get loose into the city. It is also the reason I am not asking any of you to enter, but to remain outside and dispose of any Risen or mages attempting to escape."

"So, we all go fight and lose some of our people, and the vampires get to prosper without lifting a claw?" Luka snarled.

"You all have the same right to remain neutral." Adam spread his hands in front of him. "But I urge you to stay the course. Let us not fight amongst ourselves. The vampires have agreed to track down and destroy any Risen who escape the hotel. Let that be enough this time."

Grumbling rolled through the room. I didn't blame anyone for the hard feelings, but did anyone really expect better of the undead shitheads? They chose to come back from the dead for purely selfish reasons—greed, beauty, longevity. No one became a vampire to do good deeds for millennia.

When the room settled down and expressions returned to hardened resolve, Adam tapped the glass, and it darkened once again. "Go. Rest and prepare yourselves. We move out at midnight."

CHAPTER 23

Thursday Night

Thane and I escaped to a private conference room, needing some time alone together before the battle. I knew the plan, and I knew firsthand how capable he was at keeping himself safe while beating the shit out of the motherfuckers threatening our existence. But my heart and soul screamed at me not to let this man out of my sight.

I held Thane's face in my palms and stroked the lines of his jaw with my thumbs. He held my gaze, his hands resting gently on my hips until I pulled his head down and pressed our lips together. Sparks ignited between us, exploding in my mind and body like fireworks. I tasted his warmth with my lips and tongue, amazed at the *life* that existed in this reaper.

Breathing in his sweet bergamot scent, I wanted to savor this moment forever. Deep down, I knew it would likely be our last intimate moment. Fear crept in, sending a shiver down my spine. I pressed myself closer to him, as if his mere presence could keep me safe.

Before the kiss completely swept me away, I pulled back and rested my forehead against Thane's chest, gripping his shirt in my hands. His arms wrapped around me, enclosing me in safety. I would go in with the angels, and I would find my way to his side as soon as possible. Nothing would stop me. Nothing would be able to. Our souls were connected somehow, and true death wouldn't take him from me. Not yet. I would help him earn his wings, and I would move on.

A hardness built in my stomach as my turbulent thoughts shifted to William and all the chaos he wrought in our lives. If the damn fae wasn't so greedy, Thane and I could have had so many wonderful moments together before he got his wings. So many sexy ones, too.

"Don't do anything stupid," I said, my voice muffled against his chest.

Except that wasn't what I wanted to say. I wanted to tell him how I really felt, tell him that I loved him. But fear held me back. Fear of being wrong and actually losing him, fear of having to give him up for good if I had any hope of having children. But with the other phoenix's arrival, did that even matter anymore? I wasn't the last phoenix, and I had no idea how many more existed.

Mirognya.

A deep rumble rolled through us both as the reaper chuckled, distracting me from that line of thinking before I could get my hopes up too much. "I think that warning is better directed at one stubborn phoenix."

I leaned back to give him a glare. "This stubborn phoenix has kept herself alive and free despite the repeated attempts to fix that problem."

"Seriously, Veronica." My heart always seemed to skip a beat when he said my name. His gaze danced between my eyes. "I need you to be safe. I need these beautiful eyes that always turn a shade lighter when you look at me and that stubborn heart that refuses to give up. I need to know more about what makes you tick. I need *you*…all of you."

His phone beeped just as I opened my mouth to tell him I loved him. I swallowed the words instead.

He glanced at his smartwatch and sighed. "It's time for me to prep the teams." His hands slipped down to mine, and he pulled them both up to his lips to kiss. Then he entwined his fingers with mine and led me out of the room to find the others.

Kit waited for me outside the conference room, and if the linoleum floor could talk, it would tell me my best friend was trying to pace a rut through the faux tiles. She stopped and looked up as we approached, her skin appearing a shade lighter than her usual espresso foam brown in the bright fluorescent lighting. At least, I hoped it was from the lighting.

"I need to visit my storage locker." She held up a teleportation device. "Adam lent me some wheels."

"Okay, sure." I eyed her fidgeting movements with concern. That was not like Kit. "Will you meet us back here or at the hotel?"

"I need you to come with me."

"Really?" My eyebrows shot up. I'd been dying to see her locker for years, but it was top secret. She gave me a look, one that told me I shouldn't press my luck by asking stupid questions. I turned to Thane before she could change her mind and pressed a kiss to his lips. "We'll be back in a flash."

"Be safe." He squeezed my hand before letting go so I could step up beside Kit. The man had grown wise in his dealings with me, likely knowing that arguing against me going would be futile. Besides, this mode of travel was about as safe as anyone could get.

After pressing the button to activate the teleportation circle, she took my hand and the world fell away.

I opened my eyes a second later inside one of those multi-level storage facilities, staring at an orange roll-up door numbered "117." Kit dropped my hand and tucked the t-port device in her shoulder bag, moving to the keypad.

"I feel like I'm about to enter your secret lair," I said with a giddiness I couldn't hide even if I wanted to.

"Just call me Batman." Kit finished entering the numeric sequence and stepped back. The door slid upward with a clang that echoed loudly down the empty hallway, and the single light inside flicked on.

Now, we might not have descended deep underground to a hidden cave taken over by a billionaire turned nighttime vigilante, but it would be fair to say I was *not* prepared for what I saw—which was absolutely nothing. The room was empty.

I blinked at Kit. "A far cry from Batman, don't you think?"

Rolling her eyes, she stepped inside, licked her thumb, and drew a star-like design with loops and swirls on the metal back wall. The image became visible as her thumb moved, glowing greenish-yellow in the hanging bulb's flickering light. She pressed her palm flat against the middle and uttered a command so thick with magic that it sent goosebumps up my arms. The picture faded away, the glow seeping into the wall where it slithered around to form the outline of a door complete with a knob.

My mouth parted with a slight gasp. This was some powerful as fuck magic, and while I knew Kit was an expert, I didn't realize just how much so.

"Kit…" Words failed after that because she turned the knob and pushed the door open. Beyond was a stairwell leading down into who knew where. I gulped. "Okay, Batman. Show me what you've got. Hey, does that make me Robin? Or am I more like Batgirl? She's a thing, right?"

She ignored me and entered the hidden room, which was probably for the best. My knowledge of the bat and bird heroes was limited. Extremely limited. My excited nerves were getting the best of me.

The stairwell was surrounded on all sides by solid grey concrete without a single railing in sight. I followed her down the cement stairs and into the earth, assuming that's where we were since we had been on the first level of the storage facility. But the deeper we went, the more I questioned where we were. Basements weren't exactly common in swamp-filled Florida.

The air grew staler as we descended, and the few times I put my hand on the wall, the stone was cold. I had no idea how much farther we had to go because every time I counted fifteen steps, the stairs stopped and turned ninety degrees. I lost count somewhere around ten turns, and the end was nowhere in sight. Not only that, but the lighting source only blinked to life ahead of us when we were within a few feet of the edge of darkness. It would have been impossible to see anyone—or any*thing*—coming at us until it was too late.

When the floor leveled out at last, fire came to life in sconces set along the curved walls, as if the flame leaped from one to the next until the vast cavern of a room was illuminated. My eyes widened, my eyebrows shooting for my hairline.

Now *this* was a secret lair.

Shelves upon shelves lined the rock walls, filled to overflowing with stocks of dried herbs, heaps of crystals in every hue, pots and cauldrons of various sizes, and even a broomstick. But it had a dustpan attached, so I assumed it wasn't for flying. Bummer. The lack of natural airflow this deep into the earth meant all the smells blended together into one weird mishmash, like a crockpot meal made from a bunch of leftover food found in the fridge. One of those smells you like, but you're not sure if you should.

Two butcher block tables were pushed together, barely taking up any space in the middle of the cavernous room. Each one could easily seat twelve if they were used for hosting fancy dinners. The random assortment of vials, tubing, and mortars and pestles, not to mention the lack of consistent seating, spoke to more nefarious endeavors than home cooked meals—more like home cooked magic bombs.

"Where the hell are we?" I asked, craning my neck back to try to spot the vaulted ceiling. Either it was too high up or too dark to see. A constant dripping sound came from more than one location, but no puddles of water accumulated. I wondered if the place ever flooded.

"Nowhere."

I frowned. "It's not like I'm going to tell anyone."

"No, we're literally nowhere." She pulled her multitude of braids up into a messy bun. "I created a fold in the human dimension and tucked this room inside."

So casually said, as if it were easy enough for a toddler to do. I cocked my head to the side and stood there, questioning just how little I knew of Kit's world and her abilities. "Why does it look like a cave, then?"

"The real question is why not?" She scoured the shelves for items to go in whatever spells she was going to put together. Unlike the other witches and warlocks, Kit clearly didn't plan on waiting outside the hotel for the mages to come to her—she would take the fight to them.

Returning to the tables, she got to work mixing various powders and crushing herbs and crystals together in a mortar and pestle. I stood across from her, recognizing a lilac scent before it was replaced by something funky, more like wet earth. Small bottles and vials already filled to the brim with her past creations were tucked neatly into a messenger bag designed to hold such containers without breaking them. She could pull magic straight from the elements, but catalysts like these would boost the results to fatal levels, maybe even catastrophic.

"Can you check the shelf behind you for a jar labeled mandrake root?" she asked after a quick search through the ones already on the table. "Second shelf from the bottom."

I squatted in front of the shelf in question and read through the labels: belladonna, mugwort, wormwood. Ah, there we go, mandrake.

She took the offered jar when I returned. After donning a pair of gloves, she opened the mandrake jar and removed a root with a set of metal tongs. The root shriveled and hissed when she dropped it into the mortar full of powder and continued to steam while she ground it to a pulp.

I wanted to ask her a million questions about what she was using and how everything worked, but when I opened my mouth to ask, I paused. Kit's face was deep in thought. Not just from the task at hand, but the weight of the world seemed to rest in the depths of her dark gaze and the deep valley formed between her furrowed eyebrows. Something serious was on her mind.

Her hand halted above a jar, and she looked up at me. "If things go sour, I need you to do something for me."

"Anything."

"Promise."

I let out an exasperated sigh. "Kit, you're being ridiculous. I promise I'll do whatever you need."

She pressed her lips into a thin line. "I may need you to kill me."

CHAPTER 24

Thursday Night

Ishould probably have been more specific when I said I promised to do whatever Kit needed me to do. Because I most definitely would not be killing her.

"Come again?" I asked, sure I misheard. That was the only logical explanation.

"I know it seems far-fetched right now, but if I lose control, you'll need to stop me," Kit's eyes glazed over. "Using magic can be extremely addicting."

My scalp prickled. Thane died of an overdose of human drugs, and my best friend was telling me she was addicted to magic. Was I subconsciously drawn to addicts? And then an even more ridiculous thought popped in—were addicts the only people who could love me?

I crinkled my nose. No time to let Emo Veronica out to play. "I'm not sure how addiction equals me killing you."

A shudder shook her shoulders, and her gaze refocused. "There's something I never told you about the war."

"Whatever it is, it won't change my opinion of you." I gave her a lopsided grin. "At least not enough to kill you."

She smiled, only to humor me, I was sure. "I didn't stop using magic because I was forced to kill all those people. I gave it up because..." She met my gaze, deep sadness welling in her big brown eyes. "Because, at that moment, I *enjoyed* killing them. I wanted to kill them all. The sense of power from using so much magic to basically erase a human life is indescribable."

I walked straight up to my best friend and placed my hands on her shoulders, forcing her to look up at me. "You enjoyed the magic and the power, not the killing. Addiction is a beast in its own right, making us do things and behave in ways we could never believe ourselves capable. But it doesn't define who we are."

"Yes, but—"

"No buts. You were strong enough to walk away before, you'll be even stronger now. Because now you've seen both sides, and you know you don't want the dark side."

The corner of her lip pulled up. "You have no idea you just made a Star Wars reference, do you?"

I held up my hand, palm out, and separated my middle and ring fingers to form a V.

Kit's look of disgust was palpable. "That's from Star Trek."

"Yeah? And what's this one from?" I gave her the bird, which earned a laugh.

"Veronica, seriously," she said, sobering. "I need you to help me if I lose myself again."

"I will, but not by killing you. I'll just smash you over the head with a frying pan like I tried to do to Xavier."

She raised an eyebrow. "But you failed."

Always literal, this one. "Right, but the intent was there. And if he didn't force his vampires to die in a literal blaze of glory by chomping on my leg, I would have done it."

"Just stop me however you need to if I can't stop myself." She shook her head, closed the messenger bag stuffed full of supplies, and pulled the strap over her head. "Ready?"

"Is that all you need to make?"

"For now. I'll prep more back at the agency."

"Okay, then let's head to my place so I can suit up," I said, then paused. "Wait, how will I know if you've gone too far with magic?"

She activated the t-port device and took my hand. "You'll know."

After a quick pit stop at my penthouse to change into better ass-kicking clothes and equip myself with a mini-arsenal, including my short sword Lisa and some trusty knives, we popped back to the agency. As much as I loved flying and would never willingly give it up, hopping around town via teleportation had come in super handy, with the added bonus of not leaving me ravenous.

We got back to headquarters an hour before midnight, which gave Kit plenty of time to prepare her final spells and reconnect with Angela. But because Thane was so busy with getting the reaper teams prepared, I didn't get the chance to see him again. Which, in all honesty, was probably for the best. The last thing either of us needed was a distraction or a reason to act stupid in the middle of a fight. Or at the very least, only one of us should, and that someone should be me. I didn't have wings on the line.

So when the clock struck midnight, we headed out, all shoes intact.

I met the angels on the roof and followed as they launched themselves into the air. As a bird of prey, I kept pace with them easily. The night was hot and humid, just the way I liked it. Warm air rushed beneath my wings and through the flame-colored feathers that made up the underside. The hotel wasn't far from the DEA office, but as we closed in on the high-rise building—though still a bit of a dwarf when compared to its neighbors—a light sprinkle started to fall.

Perfect. The cloud cover would help hide our approach.

We joined the ranks of silent warriors filling the forward staging location on an undeveloped plot of land behind a grocery store. Community magic kept us hidden from any human eyes; the humans who weren't part of our endeavor, anyway. As the rain continued to fall, a solemn yet determined energy rolled through the soaking wet group. Thank goodness for Miami's heat.

I stuck close to the angels, ready to follow them back into the sky once everyone arrived and Adam gave the order. But as the time dragged on, my racing thoughts drifted to what Kit said in the truck—she wanted to marry Angela. Wiping away rain from my eyes, I scanned the crowd for either of their heads with no luck. Not only was it crowded, but both women were shorter than most others here.

As excited and happy as I was for my best friend, I was also a little nervous. Maybe even scared, if the slight nausea creeping in was related to what she said. Marriage. I knew she loved Angela, but an engagement? This soon? What did that mean for our friendship I hardly knew anything about this other woman; I had only just met her for fuck's sake. Would she be jealous of our friendship and try to sabotage it? It definitely wouldn't be the first attempt by a woman Kit dated.

Even more selfishly, my whirling thoughts swerved to Thane, and I chewed on my bottom lip. Being around that reaper gave me all the feels, including happiness. But pursuing anything with him was a non-starter. Would I have to live a hundred years like Kit, or more, before I found my happy ending?

My thoughts continued to swirl around in a chaotic mess until I was jolted back to the present by movement. I snapped my gaze toward Adam just as he dropped his hand. The signal. If nothing else, I was relieved to be out of my thoughts and *doing* something again.

Once again, the angels and I launched ourselves into the air, only this time we were ready to get this ass kicking party started. As the hotel came into view, two angels broke off from the group, diving down toward the flat roof to dispatch the mages patrolling the door there. Don't let their holiness fool you—angels could and did kill just as easily as anyone else. Possibly even more so since they had their god's approval on their side.

When the roof was free of threat, the remainder of the fourteen-angel squadron dipped down to land gracefully and silently. Per Adam's plan, I would remain in the skies for another thirty minutes to ensure no other threats appeared. I was sure it was his way of trying to keep me out of the battle as much as possible. Poor guy still didn't know me very well if he thought I wouldn't do my best to kick some necromancer ass. I had a score to settle with William, after all.

I circled in the air while the angels either entered the rooftop access door or flitted down to lower-level balconies. On the ground, a ring of magical fire erupted around the hotel perimeter. A small hole in the circle allowed the wolves to run in, snarling and growling, and enclose the building entirely. The wolves took down the outside guards in a matter of seconds and rushed to secure the exits. The reapers and Kit would already be inside using their t-port devices, which became evident as windows shattered outward and bodies went flying to land in crumpled heaps or leap up and rush back in.

Battle had commenced, and so far, things were looking up for the good guys despite the fear clenching around my heart. I let out a screech, partly out of rage that this fight was even necessary and partly to calm my nerves, and prepared to dive down to join in.

A flash of color just above and to my right pulled my attention away from the hotel. Another flame-colored falcon—the other phoenix. His gaze met mine with recognition. I screeched again into the night air as he dipped and swung away into the clouds.

Oh no you don't. Not this time.

I dove after him, wings glued to my sides as I picked up speed. Through the clouds and around towering buildings, I tore after him. I would catch him and make him answer my questions. The others would be fine without my help. I was only one person, and they had plenty of fighters. I forced my thoughts away from Thane and Kit before I changed my mind.

They will be fine.

The phoenix aimed for a park with an abundance of surrounding tree coverage, most likely hoping to lose me among the leaves and branches. As usual, someone underestimated me and my level of desperation to get answers.

I reached out with my talons as we neared the dense tree line and caught him. I wrapped my wings around him just before we tumbled to the grass, and we rolled head over feet as we both shifted into human form. Landing on top of him, I had a knife to his throat before he could try anything else. There weren't any streetlights in the area, but my phoenix vision provided more than enough to make out his features.

His amused smile told me he thought he let me land on top. He wasn't that much bigger than me, the little fucker. His hood had fallen back, revealing hair the color of a raging fire and long enough to brush his shoulders. Bright green eyes twinkled under long but nearly translucent eyelashes. His skin was a lovely light caramel that came more from spending every waking moment under the sun than genetics.

As a phoenix and with such boyish features, it was next to impossible to tell his actual age, but my guess was somewhere in his first century. I admit I might have been totally wrong since I was slowly finding out how little I knew of my own kind. His coloring was all wrong besides the eyes, but a pang of familiarity gripped my heart at his playful smile—he reminded me of my brother, Maddox.

He might have been better than me in some things, but we hadn't gotten a chance to see how much and at what. So I pressed the knife deeper, though still not enough to draw blood. I didn't actually *want* to hurt or paralyze him, but I wasn't in the mood to play games, no matter who he turned out to be. "Who the fuck are you?"

"I could ask you the same." He tilted his head to the side as his gaze roved over my face.

"What's your name?"

"Ivan. You?"

"Veronica."

"You look very familiar."

I raised an eyebrow. "Because you've been following me. Why have you been stalking me? And helping me? Where did you come from?" Dazhbog above, I had so many questions.

He grinned, and the next second I found myself flat on my back, the breath knocked out of me. Ivan held out a hand to help me to my feet. Sun and flames. I didn't even see or feel the guy move. He was beyond fast. Okay, maybe he *did* let me get the upper hand when we landed.

I gave him a stern look before accepting his hand and getting to my feet. Brushing grass off my clothes and limbs, I eyed his outfit out of my periphery. Brown leather pants, a forest green leather tunic cinched with a wide brown belt, and sturdy hunting boots. His brown cloak was large enough to cover everything he wore beneath and helped him meld into our surroundings, though I wasn't sure if it was the cloak or his magic that allowed him to up and disappear outside Kit's place.

What was this guy, a Robin Hood cosplayer?

"Isn't it enough to help a beautiful woman?" He laughed when I rolled my eyes. "I didn't expect to find another *feniks* in this world."

I frowned. "A what?"

"You call it phoenix here," he said, pulling the hood back up over his hair and casting dark shadows across his features once again.

I was beyond torn. I wanted to stay and ask him all the questions I had about who he was, who *I* was, where he came from. But there was a time and place for everything, even if my impatience was trying to throttle me. I couldn't leave the Community fighting without me any longer. I couldn't leave Thane and Kit.

"Listen, I don't have time to figure all…this out just yet." I gestured at him with my hand. "The Community has gone to squash the Society of the Dead once and for all. Will you help us?"

"I'm not here to fight."

"And yet you've done just that to help me more than once," I countered.

He regarded me beneath his hood, his eyes glowing again. I wanted to ask how and why they did that, but now wasn't the time. It would only lead to more questions, and once I opened that floodgate, I wouldn't be able to close it again.

"I will help," he said, and relief settled over my shoulders. "On one condition." Of course there was a condition—nothing in this world came free. I waited for him to continue. "I need your help finding something in return."

I smiled. Finding things was my specialty. I held out a hand. "Deal."

He clasped mine, calluses scratching against my palm, and gave it a hearty shake. "Lead the way."

CHAPTER 25

Friday Before Dawn

Bodies and body parts littered the ground around the hotel as we approached by air. I took a few close swoops to determine the threat level and the best place to enter. For the most part, the pieces and parts belonged to the Risen, no longer animated with death magic. Bright flashes of light from various levels inside told me the battle was still very much in progress.

Since I missed most of the attack from above with my little detour, I spread my wings and landed in front of the main doors. They led into the lobby, where most of the fighting had come and gone already. The glass front doors were strewn in shards around the entrance and foyer. Rain quickly coated my feathers and dripped to the ground. Without the moon to light the way, the other Community members would find the world hidden in dreary darkness. Good thing I had my avian *and* phoenix vision to help me.

Ivan settled beside me, and we both shifted back into human form. My nostrils flared as the overwhelming stench of death and decay hit me full on.

"Something feels off." I withdrew two knives and gripped them tightly. "The witches and warlocks should be patrolling out here."

I ran inside, trusting that Ivan would be able to keep up and take care of himself. Hell, I should probably have made him go first, with his fast moves and all.

Other than the crunching of glass beneath our feet, the lobby was eerily quiet. Small fires lit the way from pieces of burning furniture, and clumps of paper and debris fell silently to the ground amidst the light smoke. A loud boom rocked the building, coming from a hall to the right of the reception desk. I glanced at Ivan and nodded in that direction.

As we passed a set of elevators and approached a sharp corner, I slowed, holding up a hand to keep him back while I crept toward the corner and peeked around it. A crowd faced a set of closed wooden doors with a darkened theater marquee above, and hallways extended to the left and right. A spell blocked the way through the doors, a magical barricade that resembled a wavering glass wall. As weapons or spells crashed into it, the shield lit up but remained intact, without any sense of weakening.

I caught Adam's familiar blond head near the front of the crowd and sighed in relief.

"Come on," I said and stepped around the corner.

An arrow whistled toward me, and I ducked instinctively. Fear clenched my heart as I turned to see if Ivan was hit. He held the arrow in his hand, caught right in front of his face. Holy shit, he was good.

I turned back to the group to find weapons and magic trained on us. I threw my hands up. "It's Veronica Neill and a friend!"

Adam barked an order and the weapons lowered. Damn, having brown hair really threw people off. At least it hadn't been a bullet, though it'd be cool to see if Ivan was fast enough to catch one. I had a sneaking suspicion he was.

The archangel strode over to us, his wings spread wide behind him. I wasn't sure if it was a power move like an elephant would do with his ears to warn off a predator or if he was just agitated in general. He would probably be offended if I asked, so I kept my mouth shut.

"Who is this?" he asked, appraising the newcomer.

"Ivan is another phoenix," I said. Adam's eyebrows rose, and it took me a moment to realize he was waiting for more of an explanation. I shrugged. "That's about as far as we got, but he's willing to fight with us in exchange for my help after."

Ivan and Adam stared at each other for another minute before the archangel nodded. "We welcome the help. The mages have holed up inside this movie theater and secured it with magic."

"And your magic can't break it?" I asked. Somehow that didn't seem likely.

"You forget they have fae amongst their ranks. Their magic is nearly as potent as ours. At least we are not doing this in their realm where it is strongest."

I looked around, recognizing Kit's half-shaved head and braids down the hallway to the left. But no familiar reaper. "Where's Thane?"

"Securing the upper levels, he'll—"

"I can break it," Ivan said, his attention on the wavering barrier still being blasted by Community magic.

Adam's mouth snapped shut as he shifted his gaze to the other phoenix. "The barrier?"

Ivan nodded. "With Veronica's assistance."

The angel's blue eyes widened for a brief moment, shifting between the two of us before he shook himself. "And will you?"

"Of course. I've already agreed to fight with Veronica in exchange for her help. This falls under that agreement."

"Then let us prepare for entry." Adam called out to the Community members to join us.

Reapers, witches, warlocks, and angels gathered nearby, eyeing us with cautious hope. The only ones who didn't were Kit, who narrowed her eyes suspiciously at Ivan as she studied him, and the angel Nathan, who gave me a nod of approval. Or maybe it was just a nod of hello. I couldn't really tell with him and his silent-type personality, but I liked the idea of angelic approval.

"Our new ally can bring down the barrier," Adam explained. "Spread out to all the doors and exits. As soon as it is down, we go in. Nothing has changed—your life is more valuable than any who have aligned themselves with the fae necromancer known as William and the Society of the Dead. Still, we will do our best to take them alive to answer for their crimes." The archangel nodded to Ivan, and the others dispersed to take up their positions once again.

"What about Thane and the other reapers upstairs?" I asked Adam as Ivan studied the wavering magical shield protecting the interior room.

"They will join us once the rest of the Risen have been eradicated."

I bit my lip, hating that I didn't know where Thane was or if he was hurt. I had to trust he could hold his own, and my heart told me he was alive. Having faith wasn't exactly one of my strong suits, but I would try.

Ivan took my hand, and warmth seeped through to my bones. Not the kind of heat Thane caused, but a familial bond. He was one of my kind. My pulse raced with excitement. For the first time in three years, I wasn't alone.

The phoenix led me past the group of Community members, right up to the barrier. He reached a hand up to the wavering barricade, placing his palm flat on the magical surface. "Put your free hand on it like I am."

I did as instructed. The barrier's magic tingled almost painfully beneath my fingers, and my nose begged to be scratched, but I didn't pull back.

Ivan closed his eyes and took a deep breath. His essence touched mine where our hands met, and our inner flames rose to greet each other like old friends, except mine was more like an excited child and his a patient parent. My body temperature rose as my fire magic responded to his, answering whatever call it heard.

Our bodies burst into flames. My vision went red hot, fire the only thing I saw. My ponytailed hair flew up around my head with the rush of heat, and fire ran down my limbs faster than lit oil, heading straight for the barrier. Like a torrential stream, our flames crashed against the barrier.

Beneath my fingers, cracks formed and spread in the magical wall. Ivan brought our joined hands forward and placed them on the barrier, where our conjoined fire surged once again. With a final sound like glass breaking, the whole thing exploded into nothing but thin air. Only a magical residue remained as a sulfuric scent and a brief sensation of damp skin.

We were in.

CHAPTER 26

Friday Before Dawn

Community members rushed into the open theater, running up the ramp leading inside. I stood stunned for a moment, amazed that our magic—*my* magic—had done something the others' hadn't been able to, not even the angels'. My inner flame was drained for now, flickering in and out, but I didn't even care. I still had my weapons, and we were in.

My body vibrated with excitement. There was so much more to my magic than I knew, and Ivan could be the one to tell me instead of Adam. I didn't even know how much the archangel knew about me and my abilities.

Metal clashing against metal and the boom of spells hitting targets or destroying property penetrated my thoughts and brought me back to the present. Time to kick some necro ass.

Giving Ivan a quick grin, I dropped his hand and ran inside, drawing my knives as I moved. This was what I was made for. I jogged up the red carpeted ramp, finding rows of black leather seats that reclined, complete with individual tabletops. One of those fancy, order-at-your-seat theaters. This was going to be a nice hotel. Too bad we were destroying it. Maybe I'd send an anonymous donation to help cover the damage once this was all over; we were so close to the end of this fiasco, I could almost taste it.

Stairs to my left led up to higher rows of seats and the projection room, the screen was on my right. Fights and skirmishes with Risen and mages had broken out everywhere I looked. A black-robed mage came at me with a yell, and I ducked under his staff, then kicked out with my boot. A grunt, and the mage bent over in pain. I sliced his arm with one of my knives, the quick-acting sedative doing its job as the mage slumped over the back of a nearby seat.

I had no problem killing if I needed to—I killed quite a few of these bastards already—but I still tried not to be a cold-blooded murderer. I wasn't William.

Speaking of the devil, where the fuck was that fae lunatic?

Another mage popped up in front of me, pulling my attention away from the search to block his hit. I would find the unseelie fae, I had no doubt about that. And I planned to be the one to kill him. He *deserved* death.

A terrible cracking sound rolled through the theater like ice breaking on a lake's frozen surface. I ducked instinctively just as all the doors slammed shut. The main lights went out, quickly replaced by emergency backup lighting along the floor and identifying exits. A low, vibrating hum surrounded us as new spelled barriers sprang to life at each door.

We were trapped inside.

A booming laugh echoed around the theater, sending chills down my back. I sliced the mage's arm in front of me while he was distracted, letting the sedative do the trick. Served him right for letting his own boss's plan distract him. I looked around for another Society member to take down, but it was just us left. The good guys.

"As always, the fine members of the Death Enforcement Agency are delightfully predictable." William's voice rolled through the room, amplified by magic. "You've made this gathering even easier than I expected."

My scalp prickled as every hair on my body rose. He had known about our attack. But how? Had we been betrayed? Colin wasn't back from the Otherworld yet—was he really working for the necromancer after all?

"William Caomhánach, you have been accused of grievous crimes against humanity and the Community," Adam shouted from a few rows away, his wings spreading out around him. His gaze scanned the back of the theater, but it was clear even he didn't know where the fae's voice came from. "Come and face your accusers."

"Oh, but I wouldn't dream of spoiling the show."

The main projector light flicked on, the beam directed at a single person standing in the middle of a stage erected in front of the screen. I hadn't thought much of it when I first entered, which turned out to be a mistake. Black ceremonial robes indicated he was one of the mages, pointed ears giving away his fae nature. His hair and skin were darker, more human-like than William's, so I didn't think he was from the Winter Court.

Even so, he had more natural magic than the human mages.

He raised an open hand, then used a knife held in his other to slice through his palm. He clenched his fist. As the blood flowed down his arm, he turned and drew sigils into the air, symbols that remained branded into the fabric of reality with his blood.

Panicked murmuring swept through the room, and my pulse quickened. The mage on the stage was opening a portal. But to where? I had the feeling none of us wanted to know. Time to put an end to this.

As I raised an arm to throw my knife, someone beat me to the punch. An arrow whistled through the air and crashed against an invisible barrier, splintering into hundreds of tiny pieces.

Of course. It'd be too fucking easy otherwise.

The mage continued his work, moving in a slow counterclockwise motion as he drew the sigil patterns. A new surge of mages rushed up the ramps and into the theater. With the doors spelled shut and locked, I didn't know where they came from—probably another fucking portal. I hurled my knife at a target, the blade embedding in the mage's forehead. The angel fighting that mage turned, giving me a quick nod of thanks before moving onto another target.

Like I said, I had no problem killing if I had to, and it had only gotten easier.

Ivan popped up at my side, startling me enough to jump. "We need to stop him."

"No shit. How?"

"Below." He pointed to a thin outline on the temporary stage's floor, to the mage's left. A trap door for the actors or quick scenery changes or something. Despite my flair for the dramatic, I wasn't exactly a theater nerd. "The barrier won't extend past the stage's floor. We can surprise him."

"Let's go." I followed him in a crouch down the aisle toward the side of the stage. The darkness worked in our favor, keeping us from drawing any mage's attention. The sounds of battle and blasting magic raged around me, but my focus remained on the portal. As the mage continued to draw bloody symbols in the air, lightning crackled within the circle.

We didn't have much more time.

At the stage, I followed Ivan on hands and knees behind the black curtain surrounding the structure and hiding the metal bars, crisscrossed to hold it up. Crawling beneath the stage floor was our only option since it was raised three or four feet off the ground. I was beyond thankful that the theater hadn't been used yet. Not having to deal with the floor's stickiness beneath my hands or the vomit-inducing scent of old popcorn was a minor (yet totally awesome) win.

Ivan slid the bolt off the trap door and let it drop open with the tiniest creak. He pulled himself onto the stage, his feet not making any sounds against the faux wood floor, and I pulled myself up after him.

He was right—we were inside the magical barrier. The mage was still focused on the portal, but other mages outside the barrier noticed our attempt. I raised an arm instinctively as magic came hurtling toward us, but it crashed against the shield, harmless to us inside. They rushed toward the stage.

"They're coming." I gripped my knives tighter.

Ivan closed the trap door and moved his open palm along the outline. A red-hot line followed his touch, sealing the opening shut.

"How do you still have magic?" I felt for my inner flame. It barely registered. "I'm drained."

He glanced up at me. "We'll have to work on that."

Thrills of excitement coursed through me. Yet another thing this phoenix would be able to teach me that I didn't even know was a possibility. Just how long could my magic last? And why the fuck hadn't my parents taught me whatever Ivan thought he could?

A roll of thunder sounded behind us, followed by a pop. I turned to look. The portal was open, and beyond it…

My mouth dropped open. "Dazhbog above, we're fucked."

Crowds of winged and horned demons waited beyond the yawning circle. Their eyes burned crimson and ember against leathery skin the color of ash and soot. Yellowing fangs and broken teeth grinned at us through the haze.

He'd opened a portal to hell. To motherfucking *hell*. What the actual fucking fuck?

"The only way to close it now is to get the mage through." Ivan glanced at me and grinned. "And better before any of the demons come to this side."

I nodded and ran at the mage with a yell. No sense in waiting any longer. He smiled at me and raised a hand to cast a spell as I closed in. I was expecting that, though, and he most definitely did not expect *me*. I threw myself low, sliding on one leg under his arm and just past him. Reaching back, I slid a blade across his Achilles' tendons, easily accessible thanks to his stupid sandals. He was basically begging for someone to take advantage if you asked me.

Don't mind if I do.

The mage's agonized screams rang out, and he fell to his knees. Ivan was there before I got back to my feet. He grabbed the mage by the front of his robes and tossed him toward the portal, where clawed hands gripped the edges to climb through. The mage hurtled through the opening, screaming, his hands outstretched to try to stop himself. No such luck for him. The portal was large enough for several of the beasts to fit through at the same time.

The mage's ridiculous robe came in handy after all.

As the portal lost its hold on this realm, the mob of demons inside howled in fury. They fell on the shrieking mage, tearing through his robes and skin, just as the portal shrunk to a pinpoint and disappeared. A moment later, the barrier surrounding the stage fizzled away.

With a grin, I raised my hand toward Ivan for a high-five. We made a good team.

His face contorted into a look of horror as his gaze locked onto something behind me. He pushed me to the ground, and I winced as my elbows took the brunt of my fall. I rolled over quickly and looked back. Three mages clambered onto the stage and one held a staff pointed at Ivan, whose back arched painfully, frozen in mid-air.

I ran forward to grab Ivan's foot and pull him away from his captors, only to grasp nothing but air. He and the three mages had vanished.

CHAPTER 27

Friday Before Dawn

William's taunting laugh danced around me before fading away as a bad memory. Staring at my empty hands, I felt like my chest was too tight to take a breath. The only other phoenix in this world was gone, and I had no fucking idea how they did it.

"Oh thank God, you're safe," Thane's voice was a reassuring wave as he appeared on the stage, cupping my face and kissing me.

The warmth of his touch shook me loose from the shock of seeing Ivan captured. I took a deep, shuddering breath as my lungs finally loosened. I pulled away from the reaper and grasped his hands in mine, letting the heat of his touch continue to ground me. "They got Ivan."

Thane furrowed his eyebrows. "Who's Ivan?"

Oh, right. "He's the other phoenix, and William just whisked him away somewhere instead of me. He saved my life. Now we have to save his."

"I know where William is." Thane took my hand, leading me off the stage. "We found a conference room that's been barricaded with magic, almost hidden when we ran by. I was coming back here to tell Adam when we found you all trapped inside."

It was probably the worst time to be thinking romantic thoughts, but my heart just about swelled out of my chest. Thane didn't even question my need to save this guy neither of us really knew. He just immediately jumped on board with saving him. I fucking loved this reaper.

My heart stuttered to a stop. I needed to tell Thane that I loved him, wings be damned.

Except there was no time to think about it further. We reached Adam, standing at the top of the ramp leading down toward the main exit doors, and Kit and Angela came down the steps to meet us. Being a human witch, Angela's magical and physical abilities were limited. Still, she held a gnarled wooden staff that was a good foot taller than her thanks to her petite size and carried it like she knew how to use it. She also wore Kit's messenger bag slung over a shoulder. Other than a few splatters of blood I didn't think were theirs, they both looked unscathed.

"I thought the rest of the human witchy types would be waiting outside the perimeter," I said.

"They were," Kit said. "But Angela came with the others to bring down the forcefield keeping us locked inside." She turned to look at her girlfriend, a small smile on her lips. "She's been a quick study with the staff."

"A perfect Gabrielle for my Xena." Angela leaned into Kit for a kiss.

I had no idea what she meant, but I let them have a lovebird moment before clearing my throat. "Just don't go all necro on us, okay?"

I didn't expect the joke to win any comedy awards, so it wasn't a surprise when Kit rolled her eyes and Thane smirked. But Angela laughed at my terrible attempt at humor. I liked her already; she was a keeper.

"Thank you for closing the portal before the demons could make it through." Adam's face was flushed, and the muscles along the side of his neck strained as he ground his teeth. William was in for a hell of a reckoning if the archangel got to him first, and a painful death if I did.

My heart lurched with the realization that the thanks belonged to Ivan. He was the real hero, knowing how to get inside the barrier and how to shut down the portal, and William spirited him away in my place.

"The level of blasphemy this fae and his mages are committing is beyond fathomable," Adam continued, his wings fluttering behind him. "First, the human Risen, then Raising Community members, now bringing in demons?"

Thane explained to the others where he and the rest of the reapers believed they found William.

"They also captured Ivan, the other phoenix," I jumped in when Thane finished. "We have to get him back before they harness his magic."

Adam's face darkened even further. "If William can tap into Ivan's magic and use it in his sorcery, then this world is doomed."

"Does he know you found the other room?" I asked Thane.

"Hard to tell," he said. "If he has sensors on his shields, then yes. I had to touch the barriers to know how strong they were."

"Let me guess, really fucking strong." I pursed my lips. It took Ivan and my combined magic to take down the barrier around the theater, and now Ivan was gone, and my magic was still replenishing.

"Actually, I would bet it's less so than the one that had enclosed the theater. He would've wanted us to believe he was inside the theater to lure us in."

"Okay, then let's get going," I said, stepping over a decaying and decapitated body to walk down the exit ramp.

Thane caught my hand but kept up with me, entwining his fingers with mine. The others followed as Adam barked out orders to the remaining fighters. I didn't know how many we lost, and to be honest, I wasn't ready to know yet.

"I know you don't want to hear this, but you need to stay back in this next fight," the reaper said as we entered the hallway outside the theater. "It would be devastating if they had not one but two phoenixes to draw magic from."

"You should know me better by now."

"I do, but—"

"No buts," I said firmly. "Ivan reminds me of Maddox." There. I said it out loud and met Thane's understanding gaze. "You're not stopping me from saving him."

His fingers brushed my cheek, and I leaned into the caress. Now seemed like as good a time as any to tell him how I truly felt, even if it wasn't as romantic as I'd have liked. "Thane, I—"

"Veronica!" interrupted Colin's voice. Seriously, this fae had the worst timing ever. He jogged over to us, his auburn hair more disheveled than I'd ever seen it. "Thank the gods you're safe."

I crossed my arms. "You really need to get to know me better. Trouble may find me, but I always kick its ass."

He grinned before catching sight of Thane beside me, and his smile faltered somewhat. He nodded at the reaper and turned his gaze back on me. "Prince Edric arrived just in time to make the queen listen and not banish me from the Otherworld altogether. The prince wasn't working for William; he was held captive by fae mages in the Winterlands. Thankfully, the queen listened to her son."

"Perfect timing." I tried to be cheerful, though in reality, I was still annoyed he interrupted my moment with Thane. Sure, I could just tell him I loved him at any time, throw it out there as we ran just to get it off my chest. But the damn romantic in me wanted it to be a special moment, even if fleeting. I wouldn't let William take that from me, too.

"The queen dispatched troops to fight William's mages still hiding out in the Winterlands and sent a few envoys with me to bring William in for prosecution once he's caught." Colin gestured to the three fae men with him, who looked like they had sticks stuck so far up their asses the wood would know what they had for dinner. At least the envoys had the courtesy to give me a brief glance.

Lovely people, the fae. I held back a sigh. "Let's go get the frosty bastard."

CHAPTER 28

Friday Before Dawn

When Thane said William was hiding out in a conference room, I thought he meant a DEA sized one that could hold a few dozen people. This was more like a few football fields smushed together, capable of hosting an entire technology expo or a popular comic convention. Fitting for Bill the Necromancer and his overly dramatic antics.

The angels already brought down the outer defensive barrier, granting us access inside. Not that it helped much. In fact, I almost wish they hadn't done that much.

The debilitating scent of rotten garbage threatened to expel the little I managed to eat earlier, and the incessant grumbling and shuffling of the Risen rattled against my eardrums. The mages extended a floor-to-ceiling partition that ran along the center of the massive hall, which would allow conference-goers the opportunity to set up separate, smaller rooms with additional sections. It didn't completely shut off the other side of the room, but I couldn't see past the makeshift barrier thanks to the mob of Risen who finally realized they had company.

I guessed these were simply a distraction if we got out of the theater and through the magic hiding this room. I really hoped they didn't expect us to get this far and would underestimate our determination to get to them. Even just underestimating *me* would be fabulous, because I was ready to destroy that icy fuck.

I reached for my inner flame, which was slowly crackling back to life. Not enough juice to unleash my phoenix screech on the Risen and the mages behind them. I wish I had the chance to ask Ivan even a few basic questions about the differences between our magic, or at the very least, ask how to harness it longer. No time to dwell on that now, but I was determined to get answers.

"Why don't we just blow the Risen and the partition to smithereens?" I asked Adam, raising my voice to be heard over the din. A team of reapers and angels had gone in to begin dispatching the ambling dead while we figured out the best way to attack the mages beyond. "Surely someone here has a bomb we can use."

"But what about Ivan?" Angela asked. "A bomb might kill him."

"Fire won't hurt a phoenix," I explained, semi-pleased that Kit hadn't told her girlfriend everything about me and my abilities. I might have been the last to meet her, but I looked forward to filling her in on all the juicy details of our lives.

The lines along the archangel's jaw shifted as he clenched and unclenched his teeth. "I did not want to make this public knowledge, but William was able to take another angel during the fighting. If they used the last Dagger of Abaddon, then a bomb may kill her, too."

I closed my eyes before anyone could see the fear and grief running through them. The knife in my hand trembled, and I held the blade against my leg to steady it. Killing an angel to destroy the mages wasn't something anyone wanted to do unless absolutely necessary. I had so many reasons to kill this mage, but at least I knew Jessa was still healing and safe back at the agency.

After one more deep breath, I opened my eyes and found Thane frowning. "There aren't enough bodies here for them to Raise, not en masse using an angel's power."

"Unless this hotel is built on a burial site," I joked, needing to get my mind off the sadness gripping my heart. The realization hit me that it could actually be true. I turned to Adam, my eyes wide. "Oh dear gods, it's not, is it?"

"Not to my knowledge, but Dr. Cooper confirmed that harnessing an angel's magic would allow William the ability to bring down the barrier keeping the unseelie in the Otherworld. My guess is that is his intent here."

A bucket of ice water must have been dumped over my head because everything inside me froze. I might have joked about a zombie apocalypse before, but the Risen were mindless and not terribly difficult to stop unless you were against a mob. But unseelie loosed upon the world? I shuddered. Unlike the Risen, the unseelie were far from mindless, with no qualms about destroying anyone and everything in their path and intelligent enough to predict our attempts to stop them. We couldn't let William succeed, even if it meant losing an angel in the process.

Deep snarls, growls, and a soul-shattering roar snapped my attention to the crowd of Risen. Coming from the gap between partitions, shifters of all kinds tore through the undead mob, heading straight for us. But these weren't your standard shifters—they were part of the Risen, including a motherfucking lion.

Thane's scythe snapped open in a flash. Adam barked out orders to the few reapers and angels not yet fighting to cover the sides before he joined the fray. Beside me, Kit started to chant a spell, her hands moving in the air and her eyes glowing green with earth magic. Angela dug into her bag and withdrew a bottle, which she hurled into the middle of the horde. A thick grey smoke rose around them, congealing and slowing their pace.

As I raised my hand to throw a knife, the hairs on the back of my neck stood on end. I whipped around just in time to see four dead wolves; their film-covered eyes and white bones peeking through matted patches of fur gave them away as they slunk in through the doors. What had happened to our—

My stomach flip-flopped. A reaper's mangled foot lay in the hallway outside, the rest of him nowhere to be seen. It was one thing to face undead shifters, and a whole other terrifying ballgame to face decaying werewolves. Not just because of how they looked (and smelled, ugh) with missing fur and chunks of skin hanging off their bones, but because their bite when alive could infect your bloodstream and turn you into a werewolf as well. We had yet to determine whether that ability extended after death. I sure as fuck hoped not.

Either way, the fight was on.

One of the wolves raised his head toward the ceiling and loosed a howl, which the other three picked up. The song was haunting and beautiful, almost heartbreaking as they called to a pack to which they no longer belonged.

I ducked as a wolf leaped at me, letting him sail overhead. Because Luka's pack would be securing all the exits nearby, I didn't bring any silver bullets—and who knew if they would even work on the undead. This was new territory for all of us. I drew Lisa from her sheath and spun around to face him. Just in time, too. The fucker was still fast in death, and he knocked us both to the ground with his next leap. Using my forearm, I held his snapping teeth away from my face and thrust Lisa's blade up through the bottom of his jaw until he stopped struggling.

I shoved the wolf's body off me, his bones clattering to the floor in a heap, and scrambled to my feet only to throw myself to the side to avoid another wolf attack. Slashing at his legs as I rolled, I relieved him of his front two. He fell hard on his chest but continued to push himself forward with his back legs, saliva flying from his skinless mouth as his powerful jaws snapped. I'd come back for him, but I still had two wolves to deal with, and more streamed in through the door, moving so fast they were little more than a blur— but these wolves were alive.

Luka's pack. They must have heard the Risen wolves' call. They tore through the last two dead wolves with exquisite savagery before launching themselves into the rest of the mob.

I turned my attention to finding my next target. A group of human Risen surrounded an angel, who seemed to be doing okay for the moment, so I turned my attention to an emaciated panther who was about to pounce on an unsuspecting reaper. Gripping Lisa in both hands, I approached and raised her above my head before bringing her down as hard as I could. The blade sliced through the spinal column, severing the head from the neck just before the teeth grazed the reaper's leg.

Saliva slid down the reaper's pants, but no tear. We gave each other brief nods of respect, and I turned to see the angel finish off the group of Risen.

A piercing scream made me duck my head and cringe. Before I identified the source, a human Risen came at me, arms extended and mouth opened wide for a chomp. I swung my sword up from below, taking off half her skull with one swing. A sharp, burning pain spread up my leg. I yelled out as I spun around, slicing down at the attacker's head—the wolf without front legs. I totally forgot about him.

I pulled Lisa free from his skull and checked out my leg. My pants were ripped, and blood dripped down from the bite.

Fuck fuck fuck.

I barely had any magic restored, but I pulled on the little that swirled around and sent it to the broken skin. My fire burned through the saliva trying to invade my bloodstream, cauterizing the wound before my inner flame flickered out once again. I grimaced, hoping that would be enough.

Otherwise, I might have to add werewolf to my list of abilities.

Ugh. I didn't even know what the virus would do to my phoenix genetics, and I didn't want to find out.

Free of the battle for the moment, I wiped Lisa's blade on a Risen's tattered but semi-clean shirt. A low-pitched keening sent shivers up my spine and ripped at my soul, and I whipped my head toward the sound. Between a few fighting bodies, I spotted Kit kneeling on the floor, holding something in her arms.

My lungs constricted in fear. I pushed my way through, ducking below arms and swings to reach my best friend.

Still a few feet away, I saw what I couldn't before: she held Angela's limp and bloody form to her chest. Before I was able to reach her, Kit laid the petite woman gently on the ground and stood. When she turned to face me, I paused mid-step, my heart leaping to my throat.

I no longer saw Kit in those cold, dark eyes.

CHAPTER 29

Friday Before Dawn

Kit chanted, moving her hands in the air as she prepared her magic. I didn't pay a whole lot of attention earlier at the agency when she prepped for the battle—I had my own prep to do—but now all the crystals she put on in the form of jewelry began to glow. Beads and smooth stones strung on necklaces, bracelets, and rings came to life, their colors mixing to form a rainbow of hues across her brown skin. Even her nose ring's gem shone with a green glow as she called on the magic stored within.

An orb of electricity surrounded her in red, blue, green, and white, lighting her up like a Christmas tree and electrifying any Risen unfortunate enough to get too close.

Fortunate for us, even if the reason royally sucked. Her braids rose around her head like Medusa's snakes, her eyes completely overtaken by thunder and lightning. Anywhere her gaze settled, bolts of electricity shot out from the orb, decimating whatever or whoever crossed her path.

Right now, that was mostly the Risen. But if she lost herself to the magic, then I didn't know how much longer we would be that lucky. My hands grew clammy against my sword's grip. I didn't even know she could harness the air element before now. If she turned against our allies or our friends, I would have to stop her any way I could.

"Kit!" I yelled, leaning away from a mage's swing. The end of his staff grazed my cheek, leaving a stinging mark behind. Fuck. I needed to get to Kit; I was too distracted by her to fight properly.

The ground rumbled and shook, throwing most of us off-balance, including the guy attacking me. I took that moment of distraction to stumble away toward my best friend. The earth split beneath my feet, a crack zigzagging toward her across the carpeted floor. The world heaved again, and water surged through. Kit rose into the air, supported by a geyser.

My mouth dropped open. I had known she was attuned to both fire and earth elements, but now air and water as well? How the fuck was this even possible? And why hadn't she told me?

Her gaze settled on a group of four mages grappling with an angel, and she chanted ancient words dripping with power in a deep, guttural voice. One of the mages stopped attacking the angel and turned on his peers, his eyes glazed over. He reached up bare hands to push his thumbs into another mage's eyes, crushing until blood spewed and the other mage screamed in agony. I cringed away as if that would help somehow.

Kit tilted her head back and laughed, the unnerving sound jarring down to my core. But it wasn't just the laugh that unsettled me so profoundly and made my mouth run dry. She controlled another being using the fifth element, a feat no one had accomplished for hundreds of years. The amount of magic she harnessed must have been vast. Unbelievably scary amounts.

Using the final element must be what she meant when she said I'd know she had gone too far, but there was still no chance in hell that I would kill her.

I hoped.

"Kit, stop!" I yelled from the base of the geyser, trying not to slip and fall on the uneven and broken floor that was quickly becoming a mudslide. The soles of her shoes were above my head, and the sounds of the skirmishes around us swept my feeble words away. Salty water splashed down, drenching me as I waved my arms, trying to get her attention.

Despite the noise of the room, she glanced down, recognition striking to life in her storm-fueled eyes. "Stay away, Veronica. I will end them all."

"Yes, *we* will, but not like this. Don't make me take a frying pan to that hard head of yours." I slipped on a rock and had to throw my arms out for balance to keep from falling. Me landing on my ass was not going to make this problem any more manageable, and she definitely wouldn't take me seriously if I did.

Her lip curled up in a sneer.

Oh, fuck.

I flung myself to the side as lightning struck the floor where I'd been standing, leaving behind scorched carpet and tendrils of smoke.

"For flame's sake, Kit!" I screamed, dodging another bolt. Fire I could handle, but lightning was a whole other story. I needed to figure out a way to knock some sense into her—or knock her out completely—before I became a tempting shish kebab for the Risen to gnaw on.

She turned her attention back to the mages and the partition behind them. I wasn't sure if I was relieved to not be a target anymore or pissed that she didn't consider me much of a threat.

Guttural chanting fell from her lips once again, and the air around us picked up into a rush of unnatural wind. The tornado-like gale pulled from the geyser, becoming a waterspout in the middle of the conference hall. Kit blew out her breath, her gaze locked on the partition. The maelstrom followed her breath, smashing against the man-made barrier and knocking it over, crushing the mages standing behind it.

Okay, so that was super helpful, and now I was torn: stop my bestie from going all dark and evil on us, or let her rip through the necromancers first.

When a reaper ended up singed, getting too close to a mage Kit targeted with a lightning strike, she made my decision for me.

I swiped Lisa through the geyser. The gushing water didn't stop coming, but the brief moment of disruption knocked Kit off her feet. She crashed to the broken floor beneath, and the water subsided back into the earth with a final splash. With a hair-raising growl and her gaze locked on me, she rose to her feet. Her eyes were hollow and filled with fury, all recognition of who I was gone.

This was not going well.

"Katherine Marie Parker, you stop this right now," I said, using my best mom-is-fucking-pissed voice. Of all the times I would be out of magic, it just had to be while facing my soul sister gone rogue. I needed to find a way to bring her back to herself before I was forced to do something drastic or before someone else tried to. Both scenarios were looking more and more likely.

Bolt after bolt came at me, crashing into walls and sending Risen into hundreds of bloody pieces as I dodged. Something wet and squishy splattered against my back, and I threw myself to the side again, my shoulder sizzling when one of her bolts hit a little too close to home. Hissing between my teeth, I landed on something softer than I expected. I looked down and gagged. A pile of motherfucking decaying body parts and bones had broken my fall. So fucking gross, but Kit turned her attention back on the mages.

The disgust faded. I had a lightbulb moment.

I grabbed a piece of bone—an arm bone, if my anatomy lessons paid off—and chucked it at Kit's back. It bounced off the electric orb surrounding her but also drew the electricity's attention like a static ball. I kept throwing pieces of flesh and bone, trying hard not to think about the squish between my fingers and building under my nails. The strain of defending against so many attacks at once popped the bubble shield.

With her main defense gone, I might be able to take her down.

Kit spun around to face me and let out a fierce, gut-wrenching roar. She stalked toward me, drawing water magic from a glowing blue crystal around her neck. The water swirled like two tiny cyclones in her open palms. As she neared, I dropped Lisa and the bone I picked up and raised my hands in a show of surrender.

The cyclones washed down her arms and froze into place—two gloves made of ice aimed straight at me, a phoenix who most certainly did not enjoy the cold. I let her close the distance and punch me in the face. My head whipped backward, bone-cracking beneath her frozen fist. The pain was intense, and fireworks sparkled in my vision.

Before I collapsed, she wrapped her frozen hands around my neck, squeezing and lifting me off my feet, which was quite the feat since she was three inches shorter. My broken cheek was already healing, but I choked against her hold, my body shivering from the icy touch. I had to believe she wouldn't kill me if she recognized me through the rage.

"Veronica!" Colin yelled from my left. He rushed at Kit with an outstretched palm, his magic lifting chunks of broken floor from the ground to hurl toward her.

Kit released one of her hands from my neck and held it out toward the shrapnel. They crashed against her ice glove and shattered into tiny pieces. A deep chant, and ice shards tore from her hand, knocking Colin against the wall and pinning him in place like nails through his shoulders and thighs. His scream curdled my blood.

"Kit," I choked out, "remember when Maddox died? I was lost, deep in my darkest days, but who helped me live again?"

Lightning flashed through her eyes as she tightened her hold, cutting off my breath and words. I gasped in as much air as I could, working to peel off one of her stiff fingers enough to breathe. My eyes watered from the stinging pain of the ice. "You did. You helped me find joy in life again, and I'll do the same for you, babe." I gagged as she adjusted her hold. "I will see you through this."

Kit glared at me beneath furrowed brows, but she hesitated. Did she recognize me? Was she coming back?

"Remember the letter you got from your parents last year?" A tear ran down my cheek. "Their words of chastisement and disappointment almost broke you." Her hold on my neck loosened, and confusion swam in her eyes. I kept going, "I held you while you finally told me everything. Well, almost everything. You sure held back one massive fucking secret."

The corner of her mouth twitched, and the lightning ceased striking in her eyes.

"Katherine…" That whisper of a word was all it took to shatter the final wall around her memories.

Kit's head snapped sideways to find the source, her eyes widening and returning to their familiar, dark irises. Thane held Angela in his arms, and she was still very much alive. Kit glanced back as she lowered me to the ground, sorrow and confusion vying for space in her gaze. Her lower lip trembled.

When her hands loosened from my neck and my feet touched the floor, I tilted my head in Angela's direction, patting my friend's arm. "Go," I croaked.

Her eyes filled with tears as she finally dropped her arms. "Thank you." She ran to her girlfriend's side while I crumbled to the ground, clasping my bruised and blistering neck and gasping for a deep breath. I didn't want her to see how much she hurt me.

Kit took Angela's delicate white hand, and Thane set her down gently. Tears streamed down my best friend's face. "I thought I lost you."

Angela smiled weakly. "Not a chance."

Warm hands helped me to my feet, sending tingles down my arms. "Are you okay?" Thane asked quietly.

My throat was raw inside and out but healing thanks to my phoenix genes. I knew that wasn't what he meant, though. I glanced at my best friend who was oblivious to anyone but Angela. "I'm not sure."

My best friend and soul sister tried to kill me. Sure, she warned me that she enjoyed killing people when she lost herself to magic, but I didn't think she would turn on *me*. Not after all we had been through together. But what was worse was that I wasn't enough to bring her back. She hesitated, but that didn't actually mean I broke through enough to stop her rampage. Not until she heard her girlfriend's voice.

I might have lost my best friend forever…to Angela.

CHAPTER 30

Friday Before Dawn

Wiping my cheeks with the back of a hand, I left Kit holding and rocking Angela and returned to the real matter at hand: taking down the necromancers. I would worry about my pesky emotions after this was all over.

Or I could take out a bunch of my anger on the mages. That sounded reasonable since they were the assholes responsible for making my best friend go rogue after all.

"How the fuck did William know we were coming?" I took in the devastation around us, swallowing lightly to test my healing throat, and bent to retrieve Lisa.

Thane clenched his jaw. "I have no idea, but I intend to find out."

Now that one side of the partition was down, I saw where William holed up while all the other mages were busy fighting and dying for him. The hotel's giant exposition hall held a low dais on the farthest side from where we entered. I caught sight of the fae mage's silver-white hair there, along with a handful of other mages—and Ivan.

When I saw what was there with them, I swayed with a sudden dizzy spell, nausea rolling through my stomach. Not one but *two* motherfucking portals—two massive, swirling black ovals standing upright behind William. Nothing seemed to be happening with the left, but mages entered the portal on the right and disappeared one by one.

Where in Ognebog's name were they going? More importantly, what the fuck were they doing to Ivan? His body floated a few inches off the ground, his arms and legs stiff and spread eagle, held in place by magic. His expression was locked in a grimace of pain, and tendrils of light poured from his body toward the portal on the right, entering and joining with the light swirling around the entrance.

A siphon. They were siphoning his magic to power the portal.

Colin groaned, still pinned to the wall behind me. Shit, I had totally forgotten about him. Thane and I rushed over to pull the ice shards free from his skin. He slumped against the reaper, who helped him sit against the wall to let his body heal.

A shout brought my attention back to the mages on the stage. William turned, his icy blue eyes meeting mine as if he sensed me watching. His thin-lipped smile turned sinister with recognition.

There was no way in all nine levels of hells I was going to let him get away.

I shifted into falcon form and screeched as I launched myself high into the air, diving at the Winter fae's dusky, blue-grey face, my talons outstretched and ready to destroy. He raised a hand toward me as I closed in, his bluish nails long and sharpened to points. I tumbled to the side as a fierce, ice-cold wind knocked into me. After a quick recovery, I screeched again and dove, his skin tearing beneath my talons. I continued the assault, his arms raised above his head trying to protect himself. Blood streamed down his body from the slashes in his arms and the back of his neck.

As I went for another dive, a net swooped me out of the air, and I fell hard on my side. The impact forced me to shift back into human form, and I struggled to rise in the ropes that held me. It wasn't a typical net, a fact my knife and sword quickly discovered. This was woven with magic.

Fuck.

A giant grey and white werewolf landed beside the net, moving so fast I could hardly make him out. He tore through the mages holding me down, snarling and lunging, blood splattering everywhere. Freed from the net, I jumped to my feet and threw my knife, knowing it found its mark when a mage collapsed, holding his hands to his chest.

A voice cried out, and I whirled around. William held Ivan paralyzed with magic from his staff, bringing the phoenix down from the air. Another mage ran over to attach one of their damned anti-shifting cuffs to Ivan's ankle.

William turned and stepped through the portal, Ivan trailing along behind him. They both disappeared.

I wanted to go after him, and would have, except I found the missing angel. Two mages held her limp form between them, and she was bound and gagged. A third cut away one of her wings with the last Dagger of Abaddon, blood dripping down to collect at their feet. Through my shock, puzzle pieces clicked into place. Adam said an angel's magic could bring down the barrier between the human and fae worlds, allowing the unseelie to stream through at will.

My gaze shifted to the other portal behind the captive angel. This must be a portal to the Otherworld.

A tuft of fur brushed against the fist I clenched around Lisa, and a deep growl rumbled through the werewolf as he eyed the mages. As weird as it sounded, I knew that growl from when he had found me sneaking into his bedroom to steal a ring. This was Luka, and he was ready to rip these assholes to shreds right alongside me. His lips pulled away from his teeth into a snarl, saliva dripping from his mouth.

"Let's get 'em," I said and charged at the mages.

The wolf followed.

Luka leaped onto the mage cutting away the wing, knocking him into another one holding the angel upright. The angel slumped to the ground, still unconscious, as the third mage let her go to join the fight. He swung his staff at me while chanting, but I pulled back just in time. Air whooshed by my face.

Something tugged at my leg. I let out a shout and tried to jump backward, but a thick rope wound itself around my legs and started to climb. I fell hard on my butt, wincing as pain spasmed up my back, and dropped Lisa. The tiniest flame danced inside me, barely replenished but wanting to be used. It would have to be enough, because the rope was squeezing its way up over my stomach.

I flung my arm out and sent a fireball at the mage when he opened his mouth to chant again. The fire zipped down his throat to his belly. His eyes opened wide, and he dropped the staff to hold his burning throat. A red-hot glow encompassed his entire body, and he started to melt. His skin drooped from his bones until he was nothing but a gooey puddle on the floor. With his death, the ropes binding me dropped as well. I jumped to my feet.

Luka had one of the mage's legs in his massive jaws and was shaking him back and forth while the mage screamed for help. Behind him lay the angel whose pool of blood crept toward the portal to the Otherworld. Only another inch and the unseelie would be unleashed on this world.

I jumped over the wolf and grabbed the angel's legs, pulling her away from the black hole. Another mage lay crumbled in a heap after Luka got through with him. I tore off a thick strip from the bottom of his robes to lay over the angel's blood and stop it from getting any closer to the portal.

A cracking sound ripped through the conference hall from inside the two black holes. The earth shook and rolled, nearly knocking me off my feet and freeing ceiling tiles to crumble and fall across the room. The portals were about to collapse.

Desperation fueled my steps as I stumbled across the rocking dais toward the portal to who-the-fuck-knew-where. Wherever William had taken Ivan, that was where I was headed—where I needed to go.

"Veronica!" Thane's anguished voice stopped me.

His shout tore my soul asunder. I glanced at the portal only a foot away, which was crumbling in on itself, then back at the reaper. The man who had my heart. He looked stricken as he watched me from halfway across the hall, too far away to get there in time. Fending off an attack, he moved quickly to put the mage into a sleeper hold. When the mage fell, Thane's beautiful blue eyes met mine, pleading. He knew what I was going to do, and he was asking me not to.

But I had no choice. William had taken Ivan, the only other living phoenix, captured because of me. Because he had agreed to help me. I owed him my life.

I closed my eyes, and a single teardrop slid down my cheek. When I opened my eyes again, I mouthed to Thane, "I love you."

I threw myself into the black hole just as it collapsed.

EPILOGUE

Thane

The portal winked closed, and I sank to my knees, devastation a writhing monster inside me. My chest heaved and burned as I caught my breath, though my heart grew empty. Numb.

Veronica was gone, and both portals were gone. The sounds of battle faded away as I stared at the space where the swirling black holes stood only moments before. Where *she* had been.

She loved me. That was what she said right before she threw herself inside, I was sure of it. I fell in love with that alluring phoenix weeks ago, but I never thought she would come to love me in return. Her attraction to me was obvious, but I figured that was all she would ever let it be.

But now it was too late to find out. All because of that stubborn desire to help people she tried to pretend she didn't have.

A hand settled on my shoulder and squeezed. "We will find where they went," Adam said. "And we will ensure she returns safely."

I nodded, not quite sure what I would say if I could. He must have sensed my grief and need to be alone, because he walked away to order clean up. The battle was over, a draw until we discovered where the necromancers went...*if* we ever did.

And the woman I loved with every fiber of my being was gone.

I itched at a spot on the left side of my chest—that weird red mark that showed up a few days ago.

The next day, after much needed showers and rest, Adam called me into his office. I rose from the foyer couch outside, nodding at Irene as I passed her desk. Adam's secretary winked at me knowingly behind tortoiseshell glasses. I should have felt something more than I did—elation, excitement, hell, even just okay. This was what I wanted since I accepted my role as a grim reaper.

But I didn't. I felt nothing, and the only good news right now was that I wouldn't care in just a few short hours.

"Shut the door behind you." Adam leaned against the front of his mahogany desk, arms crossed over his chest. When I approached, he stood straight to meet my eye. "Agent Munro, your exemplary service over the last five years has been noted and celebrated." Adam smiled, though it didn't reach his eyes like usual. "Your achievements in such a short amount of time will be used as training materials for new recruits, allowing them to see what they, too, are capable of achieving."

I nodded, hollow.

"You have earned your wings and then some with your handling of the Society of the Dead," he continued, "and I am honored to have you amongst our holy ranks."

I waited, knowing that this was it. The point of no return.

"But."

I blinked, clearing my gaze to focus on Adam more directly.

He smiled again. "I am willing to offer you a delay in accepting your new position."

My mouth parted in surprise. "A delay?"

"I can give you a month. If she does not return by then, you will have to make a choice: wings or your final death."

I sucked in a breath. What a gift. A month to figure out where Veronica had gone and get her back in time to say goodbye. That wasn't sarcasm, either. What I wanted was a chance to say all the things I should have already, to tell her I loved her while I still had all my human emotions intact. I wanted it to be real, to mean something. Once I accepted my wings and became an angel, my emotions would just be a shadow of what they once were. I would still love her, I was sure of that. But not in the same intense, destiny-defying way I did now.

But if she didn't return in a month, then I would have to decide whether to continue on as an angel, knowing what

I had and lost…or let it all go and embrace nothing but darkness.

I had a month.

She would come back. She had to.

I love to get to know my readers. You can reach me on Facebook, Instagram, or Twitter **@stephaniemirro**. Sign up for my mailing list to get new release information, special deals, giveaways, become a part of my ARC team, and more. I look forward to hearing from you!

www.stephaniemirro.com

Veronica's story continues in…

WINGS

OF

MAGIC

THE LAST PHOENIX: BOOK FOUR

Continue reading for a special <unedited> sneak peek.

CHAPTER 1

Friday at Dawn

Traveling through portals was not made for the phoenix kind. How did I know this? Because so far I was two-for-two when it came to traversing a frigid plane of nothingness while shivering my tits off. The last time hadn't taken nearly as long on my way to the fae realm known as the Otherworld. But I had no idea where I was headed this time, or even if some dimensions were farther than others.

Anyway, scientists might not consider two trips a reasonable number to base a statistically sound judgment, but I wasn't a fucking scientist. No, I was a walking Veronica popsicle and quite possibly lost in between realms.

My whole body shook, my teeth a clattering mess that, besides my shuffling feet, was the only other sound in this desolate wasteland. I stumbled onward through the never-ending grey mist, rubbing my hands together and blowing into them as if it would somehow help. Had I known I'd be realm-jumping today, I would have prepared by dressing smart, like wearing a jacket for starters. Too bad I had only dressed for a fight in hot and humid Miami.

The bite on my calf burned beneath the rip in my pants, which probably wasn't a good sign, but was also the least of my concerns right now. It was the only warm part of my body. I almost longed for it to spread, but I wasn't that desperate. Yet.

What kind of idiot goes running into a portal without even knowing where she would end up? Oh, that's right—*I* was that kind of an idiot. I followed William and his necromancer cronies because he had the audacity to take my new friend and the only other phoenix I had met outside my family away from me. I even left the man I loved behind.

Thane.

His name froze on my lips. I fell to my knees and curled into myself, my lungs constricting and making it hard to catch a breath. Had a breeze swept by and made it even colder? Was that even possible here, wherever here was?

Damn it all to hell. I couldn't think about leaving him, or about the devastated look on his beautiful face when he realized what I was about to do. And if my thoughts swerved to my best friend Kit and how she had almost killed me in her grief turned rage, I would be done for. I would just lie down right here and never move again.

Nope, not going there. I had to help Ivan. It was my fault William captured him. I leaned forward on hands and knees and crawled, not yet willing to give in to the possibility of being stuck in between worlds. I sure as hell wasn't ready to consider never seeing Thane again, especially not thanks to my foolishness.

My inner fire had only partly returned, and I refused to use it unless I froze in place. It was too precious to waste. But also, what good would it do if I was truly lost?

Raw and red, my fingers ached as I clutched at the ground and pulled myself forward. I couldn't even feel the grass beneath my hands anymore—

Wait. Grass?

Everything around me was a shaky blur as my entire body shivered, but I wasn't in a frozen tundra anymore. Dawn lit up the sky with widely spread golden tendrils, allowing more than enough light to see my surroundings. Leaf-filled and flowering trees reached toward the sky, explosions of color everywhere I turned. Dried seeds and pods littered the clearing around me, as did patches of vibrant green grass from where the sun peeked through the thick branches above.

I was in a forest. Holy shit. I made it, wherever *it* was. I crumbled to the ground in relief, happiness, and exhaustion. A sob escaped my lips, and I allowed my inner flame to warm me at last. I lay on my side and closed my eyes, ready to let the darkness take me while the heat defrosted my body.

Metal clashing against metal hit my ears like a thunderclap. I sat up, somehow instantly alert. The unmistakable sounds of fighting with steel made its way through the trees, along with grunts and yells as people took hits or gave them.

Ivan.

With the phoenix's name on my numb lips, which I was sure would be cracked and blue, I jumped to my feet and ran toward the clangs of battle. Adrenaline could do some crazy shit to get a body moving again, but I would definitely be paying for it later. That was a problem for future Veronica. I ducked beneath low branches and twigs, and leaves crunched beneath my feet. Some kind of weird squirrel-like animal with long ears and two tails stared at me from its perch to my right, but I didn't have time to stop and figure it out.

Ivan needed me.

I burst out of the trees and onto a dirt road. Sure enough, scuffles had broken out between the mages I'd followed from the human world and some newcomers. It was easy to tell the mages from the others since William's idiots all dressed in ridiculous floor-length black robes and carried staffs. At this point, anyone fighting against the maniacal fae necromancer and his minions was an immediate friend of mine.

Without another thought, I drew two knives and threw myself at one of the black-robed mages. I was lucky to still have the blades, having the foresight to tuck them back into their sheaths right after entering the portal. If I hadn't, chances were I would have lost them in the world between, falling from my frozen fingers.

The mage blocked my attack with his staff, and I nearly lost my footing when my knee threatened to give way. The bite mark on my leg screamed in pain. I had to ignore it for now, though, and hope someone here had some Advil or something I could take until my magic replenished enough to burn out the infection. Amputation might do the trick, too.

I sliced the mage across the arm, the quick-acting sleeping poison coated on my blade immediately taking hold. He crumpled to the side. I met one of the newcomers' gaze—a tall guy, slim, with bright blond hair and a cheeky grin. He winked sangria-hued eyes at me, a color I had never seen in eyes before. My eyebrows raised in surprise for a moment, then we both had to duck under swings.

At some point, I realized William and Ivan weren't even here, and I was pretty sure they hadn't been when I jumped into the fight. I wanted to scream a line of expletives into the air, but my vision went swirly for a moment, distracting me. I wiped sweat from my forehead before it dripped into my eyes.

The last of the mages fell with a sword through his middle, courtesy of one of the new guys. I preferred not to kill unless I absolutely had to—something that had become more common in recent days—but I certainly didn't judge others for doing so. Especially not when it came to the necromancers.

I panted and bent over with both hands on my knees as I looked around the area. The newcomers were wiping off blades and securing the few mages who survived. "Where are the other mages? The Winter Court fae?"

The tall guy who winked at me earlier frowned at me now, suspicion narrowing his strange, purplish red eyes. Like Ivan, he was dressed in mostly leather armor, only he also wore thick shoulder pauldrons and brandished a longsword. He gripped the sword's pommel tighter as he looked me up and down. "You're not human."

As a wave of nausea swept through me, I sheathed my knives. In part as a display of good faith, that I wasn't the enemy, but also because it would really suck to land on one of my own blades if I fell over. The sun's light was blinding now, and I squinted up at him, catching the hint of otherness about him and his friends now that the fight wasn't distracting me. "No shit, Sherlock. Neither are you."

"Then why are you speaking in their tongue?"

I noticed that the group of newcomers had me surrounded. Five of them, fully armed and dressed in the same type of leather armor. And only one of me in cargo pants and a tank top and most definitely not at my best. Fuck. "And what other tongue would you expect me to speak?"

"That of the *feniks*." He swept his arm toward the others. "You're one of us."

My mouth dropped open, and I tried to tilt my head to the side, only I ended up falling to my knees as my whole world spun with the head movement. "Is this *Mirognya*?"

"Of course. Are you friend or foe to the crown?" The others closed in as he questioned me.

"I… I have no idea." My breaths turned raspy, and I licked my dry lips. "I came through a portal following the mages. They took my friend. He's a phoenix. A *feniks*." Forming words was getting a bit difficult, like my tongue was swelling up. I hoped it wasn't, though, or else I might end up swallowing it. I took a deep breath. "He said his name was Ivan."

The phoenix's name sent a flurry of whispers and furtive glances among the five surrounding me. One of the others stepped forward and knelt in front of me. A woman. She had long black hair worn in dreadlocks but secured away from her face with some sort of leather tie. The olive-toned skin of her face had been covered beneath some swirly purple tribal makeup. A warrior woman. The rest of her was kind of blurry. "You're a friend of Ivan's?"

I attempted to smile, but my cheeks felt a bit sluggish. "I think so. He reminds me of my brother, Maddox." Then I fell over, my chest heaving as I struggled to get enough air.

"What's wrong with you?" she asked, her eyebrows furrowed.

"Bite on my leg. Werewolf…I think…infected…"
The world went dark.

GLOSSARY

Adam Larue – Archangel of Miami

Albert Renauldo, Dr. – human plastic surgeon; owns Star Island mansion

Angela Smith – human witch; Kit's girlfriend

Anthony "Tony" – piano shop owner; friend of Veronica

Antigone Books – eclectic 4th Avenue downtown Tucson bookstore

Ashley – Veronica's coworker at Antigone Books

Broderick Ó Faoláin – fae duke; *deceased*

Colin Ó Broin – fae double agent

Dazhbog – phoenix sun god and primary deity

Death Enforcement Agency – also known as the DEA; agency of the human world that keeps the Community safe

Drystan Neill – father of Veronica; *deceased*

El Mercado Sombra – also known as the Shadow Market

Emilia Delacroix – Master Vampiress of Miami

Enrique Alvarez – human street musician

Frank Turner – human mage; ex-necromancer

Giovanni "Joe" Facchini – fae regular of The Morning Grind; friend of Veronica

Isaac Davidson – human manager of The Morning Grind; boss of Veronica

Ivan – second phoenix

Jackson Reed – realm walker; in prison

Jessa – healing angel

Julian Delgado – Tabitha's three-year-old son

Katherine "Kit" Parker – natural born witch; best friend of Veronica

Keeper of the Forest – ancient stag of the fae woods

Luciana Pérez – natural born witch; owner of The Witch's Brew shop in *el Sombra Mercado*

Luka Navarro – alpha of the Miami werewolf pack

Maddox "Mad" Neill – brother of Veronica; *deceased*

Manuel – owner of food truck in *el Mercado Sombra*

Mirognya – unknown, possibly the phoenix realm

Mokosh – phoenix earth mother goddess

Nathan – fighting angel

Officer Harris – receptionist at prison; species unknown but most likely a troll

Ognebog – phoenix god of fire

Otherworld – fae realm, parallel to the human world

Owen Cooper, Dr. – head mortician and grim reaper at the DEA

Queen Fiadh – Summer Court queen of the Otherworld

Rhiannon Neill – mother of Veronica; *deceased*

Rico – shapeshifter; leader of the Hollow Hounds, a rogue shifter clan

Rogelio Diaz – natural born warlock; deep in his cup somewhere

Rozanica – three phoenix goddesses of fate

Sophia Clark – grim reaper agent of the DEA

Tabitha Delgado – werewolf

Thane Munro – grim reaper agent of the DEA

The Morning Grind – a DC-based coffee shop in Miami; Veronica's day job

The Witch's Brew – a witches supply shop in *el mercado sombra*

Veronica "V" Neill – the last phoenix

William Caomhánach – Winter Court fae and unseelie

Xavier Garcia – Master Vampire of Miami

ACKNOWLEDGEMENTS

To my entire family, who continue to show their never-ending love and support, *thank you*. This book (and all the others) wouldn't exist without each of you.

To my editor, Renee Dugan, *thank you*. I'm honored to have gotten to know you better over the last year, and I'm so excited for your newest adventure.

To my proofreader, Melissa Simmons; and my beta readers, Marty, Leilani, Tom, Kimmie, Jessica, Shelley, Michelle, Alisha, Rachel, Lauren, and Erica, *thank you*. Your dedication to this series keeps me motivated on the hardest of days.

To Claire Holt of Luminescence Covers, who brought Veronica to life with each amazing cover, *thank you*.

To all my family and friends, who showed their support in so many ways—asking how writing was going, becoming Patrons on Patreon, and following me on all things social media—*thank you*.

To you, my dear reader, for sticking with me and my

crazy stories about phoenix shifters and grim reapers and the shenanigans they get into, *thank you*.

This world is a better place because of books and the readers who love them.

ABOUT THE
AUTHOR

Stephanie Mirro's lifetime love of ancient mythology led to her majoring in the Classics in college, which wasn't quite as much fun as writing her own mythology stories as she did growing up. But that education, combined with an overactive imagination, being an active fantasy reader, and having a vampire obsession, resulted in the *Immortal Relics* series.

Born and raised in Southern Arizona, Stephanie now resides in Northern Virginia with her husband, two kids, and two furbabies. This thing called "seasons" is still magical.